# EINSTEIN'S

# MONSTERS

By Martin Amis

# EINSTEIN'S MONSTERS

*Martin Amis*

HARMONY BOOKS
*New York*

Published by Harmony Books, a division of Crown Publishers, Inc., 225 Park Avenue South, New York, New York 10003
HARMONY and colophon are trademarks of Crown Publishers, Inc.
Manufactured in the United States of America

Library of Congress Cataloging-in-Publication Data

Amis, Martin.
Einstein's monsters.

I. Title.
PR6051.M5E36    1987      823'.914      86-25700
ISBN 0-517-56520-X

10  9  8  7  6  5  4  3  2  1

First Edition

*To Louis and Jacob*

# AUTHOR'S

## NOTE

Some readers might like to read the introductory essay last or later. It is polemical, whereas the stories that follow were written with the usual purpose in mind: that is to say, with no purpose at all—except, I suppose, to give pleasure, various kinds of complicated pleasure. Previously I had managed only four short stories in sixteen years; these five came successively over the last two years—and then they stopped. If the stories also arouse political feelings then that is all to the good. In this debate, in this crap game, I do want to get my chip on the table, however thin, however oddly colored, however low its denomination. "Einstein's Monsters," by the way, refers to nuclear weapons but also to ourselves. We are Einstein's monsters, not fully human, not for now.

May I take the opportunity to discharge—or acknowledge—some debts? In order of composition: "The Time Disease" owes something to J. G. Ballard; "Insight at Flame Lake" to Piers and Emily Read and to Jack and Florence Phillips; "The Little Puppy That Could" to Franz Kafka and to Vladimir Nabokov; "Bujak and the Strong Force" to Saul Bellow; and "The Immortals" to Jorgé Luis Borges and to the Salman Rushdie of *Grimus*. And throughout I am grateful to Jonathan Schell, for ideas and for imagery. I don't know why he is our best writer on this subject. He is not the most stylish, perhaps, nor the most knowledgeable. But he is the most decorous and, I think, the most pertinent. He has moral accuracy; he is unerring.

M. A., London

# CONTENTS

# INTRODUCTION:

# THINKABILITY

I was born on August 25, 1949: four days later, the Russians successfully tested their first atom bomb, and *deterrence* was in place. So I had those four carefree days, which is more than my juniors ever had. I didn't really make the most of them. I spent half the time under a bubble. Even as things stood, I was born in a state of acute shock. My mother says I looked like Orson Welles in a black rage. By the fourth day I had recovered, but the world had taken a turn for the worse. It was a nuclear world. To tell you the truth, I didn't feel very well at all. I was terribly sleepy and feverish. I kept throwing up. I was given to fits of uncontrollable weeping. . . . When I was eleven or twelve the television started showing target maps of South East England: the outer bands of the home counties, the bull's-eye of London. I used to leave the room as quickly as I could. I didn't know why nuclear weapons were in my life or who had put them there. I didn't know what to do about them. I didn't want to think about them. They made me feel sick.

Now, in 1987, thirty-eight years later, I still don't know what to do about nuclear weapons. And neither does anybody else. If there are people who know, then I have not read them. The extreme alternatives are nuclear war and nuclear disarmament. Nuclear war is hard to imagine; but so is nuclear disarmament. (Nuclear war is certainly the more readily available.) One doesn't really *see* nuclear disarmament, does one? Some of the blueprints for eventual abolition—I am thinking, for example, of Anthony Kenny's "theoretical deterrence" and of Jonathan Schell's "weaponless deterrence"—are wonderfully elegant and seductive; but these authors are envisioning a political world that is as subtle, as mature, and (above all) as concerted as their own solitary deliberations. Nuclear war is seven minutes away, and might be over in an afternoon. How far away is nuclear disarmament? We are waiting. And the weapons are waiting.

What is the only provocation that could bring about the use of nuclear weapons? Nuclear weapons. What is the priority target for nuclear weapons? Nuclear weapons. What is the only established defense against nuclear weapons? Nuclear weapons. How do we prevent the use of nuclear weapons? By threatening to use nuclear weapons. And we can't get rid of nuclear weapons, because of nuclear weapons. The intransigence, it seems, is a function of the weapons themselves. Nuclear weapons can kill a human being a dozen times over in a dozen different ways; and, before death—like certain spiders, like the headlights of cars—they seem to paralyze.

Indeed they are remarkable artifacts. They derive their power from an equation: when a pound of uranium-235 is fissioned, the liberated mass within its 1,132,000,000,-000,000,000,000,000 atoms is multiplied by the speed of light squared—with the explosive force, that is to say, of 186,000 miles per second times 186,000 miles per second. Their size, their power, has no theoretical limit. They are biblical in their anger. They are clearly the worst thing that has ever happened to the planet, and they are mass-produced, and inexpensive. In a way, their most extraordinary single characteristic is that they are manmade. They distort all life and subvert all freedoms. Somehow, they give us no choice. Not a soul on earth wants them, but here they all are.

I am sick of them—I am sick of nuclear weapons. And so is everybody else. When, in my dealings with this strange subject, I have read too much or thought too long—I experience nausea, clinical nausea. In every conceivable sense (and then, synergistically, in more senses than that) nuclear weapons make you sick. What toxicity, what power, what range. They are there and I am here—they are inert, I am alive—yet still they make me want to throw up, they make me feel sick to my stomach; they make me feel as if a child

of mine has been out too long, much too long, and already
it is getting dark. This is appropriate, and good practice.
Because I will be doing a lot of that, I will be doing a lot of
throwing up, if the weapons fall and I live.

Every morning, six days a week, I leave the house and
drive a mile to the flat where I work. For seven or eight
hours I am alone. Each time I hear a sudden whining in the
air, or hear one of the more atrocious impacts of city life, or
play host to a certain kind of unwelcome thought, I can't
help wondering how it might be. Suppose I survive. Suppose my eyes aren't pouring down my face, suppose I am
untouched by the hurricane of secondary missiles that all
mortar, metal, and glass has abruptly become: suppose all
this. I shall be obliged (and it's the last thing I'll feel like
doing) to retrace that long mile home, through the fire-
storm, the remains of the thousand-mile-an-hour winds,
the warped atoms, the groveling dead. Then—God will-
ing, if I still have the strength, and, of course, if they are
still alive—I must find my wife and children and I must
kill them.

What am I to do with thoughts like these? What is
anyone to do with thoughts like these?


Although we don't know what to do about nuclear weapons,
or how to live with nuclear weapons, we are slowly learning
how to write about them. Questions of decorum present
themselves with a force not found elsewhere. It is the high-
est subject and it is the lowest subject. It is disgraceful, and
exalted. Everywhere you look there is great irony: tragic

irony, pathetic irony, even the irony of black comedy or farce; and there is irony that is simply violent, unprecedentedly violent. The mushroom cloud above Hiroshima was a beautiful spectacle, even though it owed its color to a kiloton of human blood. . . .

In the discursive sphere there are several ways of writing badly about nuclear weapons. Some people, you finally conclude, just don't get it. They just don't get it. They are published versions of those bus-stop raconteurs who claim that nuclear war won't be "that bad," especially if they can make it down to their aunt's cottage in Dorset (or, better still, if they are already in their aunt's cottage at the time). They do not see the way nuclear weapons put everything into italic capitals. Failing to get the point about nuclear weapons is like failing to get the point about human life. This, in fact, is the basis of our difficulty.

It is gratifying in a way that all military-industrial writing about nuclear "options" should be instantly denatured by the nature of the weapons it describes, as if language itself were refusing to cooperate with such notions. (In this sense language is a lot more fastidious than reality, which has doggedly accepted the antireality of the nuclear age.) In the can-do world of nuclear "conflict management," we hear talk of *retaliating first;* in this world, deaths in the lower tens of millions are called *acceptable;* in this world, hostile, provocative, destabilizing nuclear weapons are aimed at nuclear weapons *(counterforce),* while peaceful, defensive, security-conscious nuclear weapons (there they languish, adorably pouting) are aimed at cities *(countervalue).* In this world, opponents of the current reality are known as *cranks.* "Deceptive basing modes," "dense pack groupings," "baseline terminal defense," "the Football" (i.e., the Button), acronyms like BAMBI, SAINTS, PALS, and AWDREY (Atomic Weapons Detection, Recognition, and Estimation of Yield), "the Jedi concept" (near-lightspeed plasma weapons), "Star Wars" itself: these locutions take you out onto the sports field—or back to the nursery.

In fact there is a resilient theme of infantilism throughout the history of nuclear management. Trinity, the first bomb (nicknamed the Gadget), was winched up into position on a contraption known as "the cradle"; during the countdown the Los Alamos radio station broadcast a lullaby, Tchaikovsky's "Serenade for Strings"; scientists speculated whether the Gadget was going to be a "girl" (i.e., a dud) or a "boy" (i.e., a device that might obliterate New Mexico). The Hiroshima bomb was called Little Boy. "It's a boy!" pronounced Edward Teller, the "father" of the H-bomb, when "Mike" ("my baby") was detonated over Bikini Atoll in 1952. . . . It is ironic, because *they* are the little boys; *we* are the little boys. And the irony has since redoubled. By threatening extinction, the ultimate antipersonnel device is in essence an antibaby device. One is not referring here to the babies who will die but to the babies who will never be born, those that are queueing up in spectral relays until the end of time.

I first became interested in nuclear weapons during the summer of 1984. Well, I say I "became" interested, but really I was interested all along. Everyone is interested in nuclear weapons, even those people who affirm and actually believe that they never give the question a moment's thought. We are all interested parties. Is it possible never to think about nuclear weapons? If you give no thought to nuclear weapons, if you give no thought to the most momentous development in the history of the species, then what *are* you giving them? In that case the process, the seepage, is perhaps preconceptual, physiological, glandular. The man with the cocked gun in his mouth may boast that he never thinks about the cocked gun. But he tastes it, all the time.

My interest in nuclear weapons was the result of a coincidence. The two elements were impending fatherhood and a tardy reading of Jonathan Schell's classic, awakening study, *The Fate of the Earth*. It woke *me* up. Until then, it seems, I had been out cold. I hadn't really thought about nuclear weapons. I had just been tasting them. Now at last I knew what was making me feel so sick.

How do things go when morality bottoms out at the top? Our leaders maintain the means to perform the unthinkable. They contemplate the unthinkable, on our behalf. We hope, modestly enough, to get through life without being murdered; rather more confidently, we hope to get through life without murdering anybody ourselves. Nuclear weapons take such matters out of our hands: we may die, and die with butcher's aprons around our waists. I believe that many of the deformations and perversities of the modern setting are related to—and are certainly dwarfed by—this massive preemption. Our moral contracts are inevitably weakened, and in unpredictable ways. After all, what *acte gratuit,* what vulgar outrage or moronic barbarity can compare with the black dream of nuclear exchange?

Against the hyperinflation of death that has cheapened all life, it is salutary to return to the physics, to remind ourselves about nuclear *scale.* The amount of mass expended in the razing of Hiroshima was about a thirtieth of an ounce— no heavier than a centime. In accordance with Einstein's equation, a single gram assumed the properties of 12,500 tons of TNT (together with certain properties of its own). This is Jonathan Schell:

> . . . the energy yielded by application of the universal physics of the twentieth century exceeds the energy yielded by that of the terrestrial, or planetary, physics of the nineteenth century as the cosmos exceeds the earth. Yet it was within the earth's comparatively tiny, frail ecosphere that mankind released the newly tapped cosmic energy.

Let us ignore, for a moment, the gigaton gigantism of present-day arsenals and reflect on what a single megaton could do: it could visit Hiroshima-scale destruction on every state capital in America, with about thirty bombs to spare. The Soviet arsenal alone could kill approximately twenty-two billion people—or it could if there were twenty-two billion people around to kill. But there are only four billion people around to kill. And still we pursue the dynamic rationale of the missile gap. There is no *gap.* We live in a

Manhattan of missiles. Rather, there is no room. We are full up.

Meanwhile the debate goes on. And what kind of debate is it? What is its tone? If we look at the controversy over the Strategic Defense Initiative we find that this, for instance, is Ronald Reagan's tone: "[SDI] isn't about fear, it's about hope, and in that struggle, if you will pardon my stealing a film line, the Force is with us." No, we will not pardon his stealing a film line. And the Force is not with us. The Force is against us. In such terms, at any rate (terms that aspire to an infinite frivolity), President Reagan entrained "an effort which holds the promise of changing the course of human history," but which also, he allowed, involved "risks." Unfortunately the risk is that of *ending* the course of human history. "God will not forgive us if we fail," Brezhnev told Carter at the pre-Afghanistan summit. Carter liked the phrase and used it himself, with one politic emendation. "History," he said, "will not forgive us if we fail." Actually Brezhnev was nearer the mark. In the event of "failure," God might just make it, whereas history would not.

Three books on SDI—three quickies on the end of time —have recently landed on my desk, two pro and one anti. *How to Make Nuclear Weapons Obsolete* is by Robert Jastrow, the man who jumped into newsprint the day after the space-shuttle disaster with the comment, "It's almost fishy." First, Jastrow makes it clear how much he hopes that World War III can, if possible, be avoided, how much he would regret and deplore such an eventuality (the tone is the familiar one of hurried moral gentrification, as if this were all a wearisome matter of etiquette and appearances); he then addresses himself to the main business of the book, a stirred account of "The Battle." Here in the midst of the techno-philiac space-opera we glimpse the president coolly "order-ing" this and "deciding" that, coolly erecting his untried "peace shield" as hemispherical butchery looms in the skies above. In fact the president, if he has not been vaporized by a suitcase bomb in the Russian embassy, will be understand-ably immersed in his own nervous breakdown, along with every other actor in this psychotic fantasy. For Jastrow, the unthinkable is thinkable. He is wrong, and in this respect he is also, I contend, subhuman, like all the nuclear-war fighters, like all the "prevailers." The unthinkable is un-thinkable; the unthinkable is not thinkable, not by human beings, because the eventuality it posits is one in which all human contexts would have already vanished. SDI can never be tested, and neither can the actors. How they would respond at such a time is anyone's guess. But they would no longer be human beings. In a sense, nobody would be. That status does not exist on the other side of the firebreak.

Solly Zuckerman has suggested that the Allies' complai-sance on SDI, lukewarm and hangdog though it was, could not have survived a reading of Jastrow. Probably the same could not be said for Alun Chalfont, whose *Star Wars: Sui-cide or Survival?* welcomes SDI in the baritone of gruff real-ism. True, the Initiative will entail "high risk"; true, the Initiative "calls for an entirely new approach to the doctrines underlying arms control policies"; true, the Initiative will cost a trillion dollars. But it's worth it. Highly risky, en-tirely revolutionary, and incredibly expensive, it's worth it —because of the Gap. The Soviets will soon be doing it, or have started doing it, or (he sometimes seems to suggest) have already done it. So we'd better do it too. . . . Interestingly, what exercises Lord Chalfont is not the existence of nuclear weapons, an existence which, he says, cannot be "repealed."* What exercises Lord Chalfont is the existence of their opponents. Now here is something we *can* get rid of. Civility, in any case, absents itself from his prose whenever the subject of peace—or "peace"—is wearily introduced. "Immediately the peace industry begins its predictable uproar . . . a coalition of misguided idealists, with a sprinkling of useful idiots and Soviet agents (conscious and unconscious)." Annoyed by references to the war "industry," he nonetheless accords industrial status to the peace movement. Why? Where are the factory townships of peace? Where are its trillion-dollar budgets? At one point Chalfont discusses American plans

for the deployment of enhanced radiation warheads in Europe . . . there is, at once, an uproar against the "neutron

---

* Endorsing America's recently tightened embrace of the nuclear destiny, Margaret Thatcher has echoed this line, claiming that "nuclear weapons can't be uninvented" —an "unimpeachable point," according to *The Times*. (*The Times,* like *The Economist,* like *The Sun,* is incidentally pro-SDI.) With the assistance of Jonathan Schell's *The Abolition,* may I put this argument out of its misery? It is true that nuclear weapons cannot be uninvented (or better say undiscovered, since they utilize an eternal force of nature); but they can be dismantled. If nuclear weapons are used, they will be used by a lunatic or by a sane man in a crisis. Any appreciable extension of the second-thoughts period would be of epochal significance: it would make a new world. Currently the second-thoughts period is the time that elapses between deciding to press a button and actually pressing it. President Reagan himself seemed to feel the need for greater respite when, after some years in power, he announced his belief that the missiles, once launched, could be recalled. Bullets cannot be recalled. They cannot be uninvented. But they can be taken out of the gun.

bomb"—described by the mentally enfeebled as a capitalist weapon, designed to kill people but preserve property.

Chalfont isn't happy with the phrase "capitalist weapon,"
and one concurs. But how happy is he with "enhanced
radiation warheads"? How happy is he with "enhanced"?
E. P. Thompson is unfortunately not much nearer to
finding the voice of appropriate and reliable suasion. He has
made great sacrifices for the cause he leads; he is brilliant,
he is charismatic, he is inspiring; but he is not reliable. In
*Star Wars,* as elsewhere, Professor Thompson shows himself
to be the fit exponent of the nuclear High Style. He is witty
and grand, writing with the best kind of regulated hatred.
How devastating he is, for example, on the SDI public-
relations effort. From the confidential literature:

> Innumberable opportunities for highly visible "cause" ac
> tivism could be opened up . . . interest to Catholics also.
> . . . Such a ratification effort would permit the White
> House to look good in confronting powerful anti-BMD
> domestic critics . . . addresses "Eurostrategic" issues,
> which are big today . . . play freely on high-road ethical
> themes (by far the best mobilizational approach) . . .

Thompson is devastating about SDI; his case is well-nigh
complete. But he will devastate nobody—indeed, he may
even subvert the converted—because he has no respect for
tone.

His tone is lax, impatient, often desperately uncertain; it
is excitedly alarmist; it takes pleasure in stupidity. His anti-
Americanism ("the US of A is inherently moral," "President
of Planet Earth," "I want you Commies to come out with

your hands up") is as dated and grueling, and as much a
matter of stock response, as the counterprejudices of Lord
Chalfont. Thompson also makes jokes. He likes this joke so
well that he cracks it twice:

> Already, the soon-to-be President warned, the window [of
> vulnerability] might be so wide open that "the Russians
> could just take us with a phone call." "Hallo! Mr. Reagan,
> is zat you? Tovarich Brezhnev here. Come on out with
> your hands up, or I put zis Bomb through the window!"

Everything in you recoils from this. You sit back and rub
your eyes, wondering how much damage it has done. For
in the nuclear debate, as in no other, the penalty for such
lapses is incalculable. Human beings are unanimous about
nuclear weapons; human institutions are not. Our hopes
lie in a gradual symbiosis. We must find the language
of unanimity.


I argue with my father about nuclear weapons. In this debate, we are all arguing with our fathers. They emplaced or
maintained the status quo. They got it hugely wrong. They
failed to see the nature of what they were dealing with—
the nature of the weapons—and now they are trapped in the
new reality, trapped in the great mistake. Perhaps there
will be no hope until they are gone. Out on the fringes there
are people who believe that we ought to start killing certain
of our fathers, before they kill us. This reminds me of the
noble syllogism (adduced by Schell) of Failed Deterrence:
"He, thinking I was about to kill him in self-defense, was

about to kill me in self-defense. So I killed him in self-defense." Yes, and then he killed me in retaliation, from the grave. Our inherited reality is infinitely humiliating. We must try to do a little better.

My father regards nuclear weapons as an unbudgeable given. They will always be necessary because the Soviets will always have them and the Soviets will always want to enslave the West. Arms agreements are no good because the Soviets will always cheat. Unilateral disarmament equals surrender. And anyway, it isn't a case of "red or dead." The communist world is itself nuclear-armed and deeply divided: so it's a case of "red *and* dead."

Well, *dead,* at any rate, is what this prescription seems to me to promise. Nuclear weapons, my father reminds me, have deterred war for forty years. I remind him that no global abattoir presided over the century-long peace that followed Napoleon's discomfiture in 1815. And the trouble with deterrence is that it can't last out the necessary time-span, which is roughly between now and the death of the sun. Already it is falling apart from within. When I say that America is as much of a threat as the Soviet Union my father categorizes me as someone who takes democracy lightly, who takes freedom lightly. But of course it is the weapons themselves that are the threat. Ironically, an autocracy is much the better equipped to deal with this question, because the question is superpolitical. There is no one for the Soviets to deal with—leaders of sharply deteriorating caliber, beset by democracy, by politics, and doing six-month stints between midterm elections, lame-duck periods, and the informal referenda of American public life. And there is money, the money. It would seem, at the time of writing, that the Soviet Union can't afford to go on and that the United States can't afford to stop. Saul Bellow has written that there are certain evils—war and money are the examples he gives—that have the power to survive identification as evils. They cheerfully continue, as evils, as known evils. Could it be a further accomplishment of nuclear weapons that they have united these continuations, in a process of terminal decay? So the world ends in the same way *The Pardoner's Tale* ends, with the human actors gone, leaving behind (though no one will find them) the spent weapons and the unspent money, the weapons and the money.

Anyone who has read my father's work will have some idea of what he is like to argue with. When I told him that I was writing about nuclear weapons, he said, with a lilt, "Ah. I suppose you're . . . 'against them,' are you?" *Epater les bien-pensants* is his rule. (Once, having been informed by a friend of mine that an endangered breed of whales was being systematically turned into soap, he replied, "It sounds like quite a good way of *using up* whales." Actually he likes whales, I think, but that's not the point.) I am reliably ruder to my father on the subject of nuclear weapons than on any other, ruder than I have been to him since my teenage years. I usually end by saying something like, "Well, we'll just have to wait until you old *bastards* die off one by one." He usually ends by saying something like, "Think of it. Just by closing down the Arts Council we could significantly augment our arsenal. The grants to poets could service a nuclear submarine for a year. The money spent on a *single* performance of *Rosenkavalier* might buy us an extra neutron warhead. If we closed down all the hospitals in London we could . . ." The satire is accurate in a way, for I am merely going on about nuclear weapons; I don't know what to do about them.

We abandon the subject. Our sessions end amicably. We fall to admiring my one-year-old son. Perhaps he will know what to do about nuclear weapons. I, too, will have to die off. Perhaps he will know what to do about them. It will have to be very radical, because there is nothing more radical than a nuclear weapon and what *it* can do.

Another satirical voice in the debate is that of Civil Defense. Unlike Professor Thompson's, these jokes *are* funny. *Civil Defense Against Nuclear Attack*—the concept is a joke in itself. There are only two words to be said, and they are *forget it.* Nevertheless, books on this subject continue to appear. I suppose someone has to write them, but the whole genre is scuppered by subhuman bathos. It is like trying to acquaint the Royal Family with the consolations of life in a blood-soaked lean-to, or a medieval field hospital. (And, against this particular backdrop, every family is a royal family.) In the nuclear hospital, by another feral irony, there will be a reversed triage: only the comparatively healthy are considered treatable. The process of nuclear inversion is complete when one realizes that the correct attitude to nuclear war is one of suicidal defeatism. Let no one think that it is thinkable. Dispel any interest in surviving, in lasting. Have no part of it. Be ready to turn in your hand. For myself and my loved ones, I want the heat, which comes at the speed of light. I don't want to have to hang about for the blast, which idles along at the speed of sound. There is only one defense against nuclear attack, and that is a cyanide pill.

Recently I came across an American offering, *Civil Defense in Nuclear Attack: A Family Protection Guide* by Capt. T. Kalogroulis. It is a peach. It is also full of illiteracies and misprints ("A schematic illustration of the blast wave is shown in the neat page?"). But I imagine we can live with that. After a nuclear attack, I imagine we can live with a few misprints. The book begins with the Justification—the justification for all this ghoulish prattle. "The Communist aim is world domination . . . they will use nuclear blackmail based on their boasted capabilities. And they are prepared to use force if they need to and can afford the risk." That *if* is not a big one, because the Soviets "might accept a risk in human and property losses that we would not consider risking. They are hardened to losses." The enemy is not made of flesh and blood but of hide and ice; to them, nuclear holocausts are meat and drink. Over the page, Captain Kalogroulis lists the "strategic advantages of population protection." There are seven of them. Number four states that "protection of the people gives meaning to all military defense; the latter has no meaning if the populations perishes." What meaning does the former have, if the population perishes? Here is number five:

Our leading military authorities agree that ability to limit our casualties in event of an attack has definite military advantages. It would mean that an enemy must commit greater military and economic strength to the venture. It would thus take him longer to attain capability.

In other words, the enemy would have to go to extra trouble in rendering the casualties *un*limited. One wonders, too, how much clout and prestige our leading military authorities would really enjoy, "in event of an attack." Number seven concludes that population protection "creates ability to endure a nuclear war." One is obliged to pull through, then, for strategic reasons.

The clear truth is that after a nuclear war the role of the civil and military establishment would change or invert. The authorities would no longer be protecting the population from the enemy: they would be protecting themselves from the population. One of the effects of nuclear weapons —these strange instruments—would be instant fascism. In 1980 the British government conducted Operation Square Leg, in conjunction with NATO, to assess the realities of nuclear attack. Together with many other mysterious assumptions (seven-day warning, no detonation in central London), it is imagined that the populace would spend its last week stocking up with food and turning its back gardens into shelters—in other words, digging its own grave. Because when you stagger out of your shelter, following the "All Clear" (all clear for what?), the only thing worth doing would be to stagger back in again. Everything good would be gone. You would be a citizen of a new town called Necropolis. Nuclear civil defense is a nonsubject, a mischievous fabrication. It bolsters fightability. It bolsters thinkability.

For all its black slapstick, however, the genre has a plangent undertow. Not everyone (by definition) is as thoroughly, as exemplarily subhuman as Captain Necropolis. The admirable *London After the Bomb,* for instance, starts off as a book "about" nuclear defense and ends up as a disgusted rejection of nuclear defense. Even with semiofficial publications like *Nuclear Attack: Civil Defence* (Commissioned and Edited by the Royal United Services Institute for Defence Studies) you get the following impression: that of a team of experienced paramedics, well prepared for a vicious assault on their senses, who then find themselves reeling from the scene of the accident, in helpless nausea. Language cannot live with this reality. "It is important to have a good supply of painkillers . . . tranquilizers will be important . . . psychological problems in a nuclear war . . . health problems in a nuclear war . . ." Is *problems* really the word we want? Well, there will be extinction problems too, as— with aspirin tablets, four-by-four-inch sterile pads, small scissors (blunt ended) and a provident supply of safety pins —we hunker down for the nuclear winter.

Nuclear winter has been the best news on this front since 1945. It is the best news because it is the worst news (and because nuclear realities are always antithetical or palindromic). To put the matter simply, if a considerable fraction of the world's arsenals were used, the planet might cease to support life. Thus even a successful first strike might fatally redound upon the attacker. It took nearly forty years to grasp an obvious truth: that there is no fire without smoke. How long will it take us to grasp that nuclear weapons are not weapons, that they are slashed wrists, gas-filled rooms, global booby traps? What more do we need to learn about them? Some people—and it does take all sorts, to make a world—are skeptical about nuclear winter; extinction is something they feel they can safely pooh-pooh. Certainly the case is not proven: like every other nuclear ramification, it pullulates with uncertainty. (The chemistry of ozone creation and destruction, for example, is only partially understood.) But the pessimistic view would seem to me to be the natural one. Where are the hidden pluses, where are the pleasant surprises, when it comes to nuclear weapons? Anyway, the ethical argument remains watertight. If the risk is infinite—as Schell points out in *The Fate of the Earth*—a scientific possibility can be treated as a moral certainty, "because if we lose, the game will be over, and neither we nor anyone else will ever get another chance." Or, as he puts it in his later book, *The Abolition:*

> For now human beings, engaged, as always, in the ambitions and disputes of their particular place and time, can end the human story in all places for all time. The eternal has been placed at stake in the temporal realm, and the infinite has been delivered into the care of finite human beings.

And it makes imaginative sense, I think, that the enchanting mysteries of matter, of quanta, should encode an ending (the atom itself being no more than a set of relationships). Mathematically the universe is a fluke. So is the earth, this blue planet, and so is organic life. Though each confirmation is welcome, we do not need the Friends of the Earth or *The Tao of Physics* to tell us that in our biosphere everything is to do with everything else. In that they are human, all human beings feel it—the balance, the delicacy. We have only one planet, and it is *round*.

The central concept in nuclear-winter theory is *synergism*. When two bad things happen, a third (and unpredictable) bad thing happens, exceeding the sum of the individual effects. This is on top of the bad things we know a good deal about, already quite a list. Prompt radiation, superstellar temperatures, electromagnetic pulse, thermal pulse, blast overpressure, fallout, disease, loss of immunity, cold, dark, contamination, inherited deformity, ozone depletion: with what hysterical ferocity, with what farcical disproportion, do nuclear weapons loathe human life. . . . It is possible to imagine nuclear synergisms multiplying into eternity, popping and crackling away, inimical to life even when there is nothing left to be inimical to. The theory of nuclear winter was prompted by studies of dust storms on Mars, and Mars gives us a plausible vision of a postnuclear world. It is vulcanized, oxidized, sterilized. It *is* the planet of war.

Soon after I realized I was writing about nuclear weapons (and the realization took quite a while: roughly half of what follows in this book was written in innocence of its common theme), I further realized that in a sense I had been writing about them all along. Our time is different. All times are different, but our time is *different*. A new fall, an infinite fall, underlies the usual—indeed traditional—presentiments of decline. To take only one example, this would help explain why something seems to have gone wrong with time

—with modern time; the past and the future, equally threatened, equally cheapened, now huddle in the present. The present feels narrower, the present feels straitened, discrepant, as the planet lives from day to day. It has been said —Bellow again—that the modern situation is one of *suspense:* no one, no one at all, has any idea how things will turn out. What we are experiencing, in as much as it can be experienced, is the experience of nuclear war. Because the anticipation—Schell again—the anxiety, the suspense, is the only experience of nuclear war that anyone is going to get. The reality (different kinds of death, in a world without discourse) could hardly be called human experience, any more than such temporary sentience as remained could be called human life. It would just be human death. So this is it, this is nuclear war—and it is ruining everything. The "effects" of nuclear weapons have been exhaustively studied, though of course nobody will ever know their full extent. What are the psychological effects of nuclear weapons? As yet undetonated, the world's arsenals are already waging psychological warfare; deterrence itself, for instance, is entirely psychological (and, for that reason, entirely inexact). The airbursts, the preemptive strikes, the massive retaliations, the uncontrollable escalations: it is already happening inside our heads. If you think about nuclear weapons, you feel sick. If you don't think about them, you feel sick without knowing why. Nuclear weapons repel all thought, perhaps because they can end all thought.

For some reason, and it is no doubt an intriguing reason, the bulk of imaginative fiction on the subject belongs to the genres. Pentagon-and-Kremlin countdowns, terrorist or rogue-leader nail-biters, love and pain in the postapocalyptic tundra. Science fiction started concerning itself with doomsday weapons long before such weapons were ever mooted, and nowadays about one SF novel in four is set beyond the holocaust. Meanwhile, it is astonishing how little the mainstream has had to say about the nuclear destiny—a destiny that does not want for complication, inclusiveness, pattern, paradox, that does not want for *interest*. (Nuclear weapons have many demerits, but drabness is not one of them.) And yet the senior generation of writers has remained silent; prolific and major though many of them are, with writing lives that straddled the evolutionary firebreak of 1945, they evidently did not find that the subject suggested itself naturally. They lived in one kind of world, then they lived in another kind of world; and they didn't tell us what the difference was like. I recently asked Graham Greene what the difference was like, and he said that he had never really thought about it. I do not count this as any kind of defeat for Graham Greene, the most prescient writer of our time. But I do count it as some kind of victory for nuclear weapons.

Clearly a literary theme cannot be selected, cannot be willed; it must come along at its own pace. Younger writers, writers who have lived their lives on the other side of the firebreak, are beginning to write about nuclear weapons. My impression is that the subject resists frontal assault. For myself, I feel it as a background, a background which then insidiously foregrounds itself. Maybe the next generation will go further; maybe the next generation will be more at home with the end of the world. . . . Besides, it could be argued that all writing—all art, in all times—has a bearing on nuclear weapons, in two important respects. Art celebrates life and not the other thing, not the opposite of life. And art raises the stakes, increasing the store of what might be lost.

Mutual Assured Destruction: it sounds like an insurance firm or a building society until we reach its final element. *Will* we reach its final element? MAD is a disgusting and ridiculous doctrine, and a desire to escape from it has now given us SDI. I had been reading the pro-SDI literature for quite some time when, sure enough, I finally came across something to be said for it. It might lessen the slaughter of an *accidental* war. The next day I read Daniel Ford's brilliant book, *The Button,* and learned that accidental war is something that many of the fiercest critics of nuclear policy now utterly discount. So SDI has nothing to be said for it. Arms improvement is the very crux of the present danger. A new emphasis on defense combined with arms reduction and obsolescence is a possible future. A new emphasis on defense combined with the status quo is just more of the same. It is just more weapons. Weapons are like money: no one knows the meaning of *enough.* If we could look at ourselves from anything approaching the vantage of cosmic time, if we had any sense of cosmic power, cosmic delicacy, then every indicator would point the same way: *down.* Down, down, down. We do not need this new direction, which is *up.*

In *The Logic of Deterrence,* Anthony Kenny, a philosopher and former priest, is unfailingly apposite in his search for moral breathing space in the nuclear world. In terms of ethics, justice, and humanity, deterrence is a ruin; it is unsurprising that it has no logic either. A first strike is morally impossible. But so is a second strike. Deterrence having failed, it cannot be effected retroactively by retaliation. Schell makes the point very neatly:

> . . . there is nothing that it would make sense to do "if deterrence fails" . . . When the President is asked what the United States will do if it is subjected to nuclear attack by the Soviet Union, he cannot answer, "I will immediately call up the Soviet Premier and ask him to please stop." He cannot tell the world that if we suffer nuclear attack our retaliation will be a phone call. For the instant he gave that answer deterrence would dissolve.

Generally it is encouraging to see the weight of the churches being enlisted toward the utopian unanimity, in the form of papal statements, pastoral letters, responsible activism, and so on. But nuclear weapons are mirrors in which we see all the versions of the human shape. Incomparably the most influential religious body on earth, the New Evangelicals, who exercise real power, warmly anticipate "a holy nuclear war," which will exalt Israel (where the hostilities begin) and crush Russia, before going on to dramatize the Apocalypse. These people are Born Again; and they seem to want to Die Again. A "holy" nuclear war: here we stare into the foundry of the moronic inferno, an inferno that is one of our possible futures.

I write these words in Israel. Our group has just visited the
Museum of the Holocaust. Our group has just climbed
Masada. "Masada": whereas the historicity of the Masada
story remains uncertain, its mythopoeic importance to the
Jewish idea is clear enough. (Hence "the Masada complex,"
in fact a hawkish formulation used to shore up Israeli maxi-
malism.) Suppression, revolt, beleaguerment, mass suicide
—sacrifice. A holocaust is a sacrifice, "a sacrifice wholly
consumed by fire . . . a whole burnt offering . . . a complete sacrifice."

The northern view from the monstrous boulder of Masada
is one of elemental beauty. It makes you feel what it is to
live on a planet; it makes you feel what it is to live on a
larger, emptier, cleaner, and more innocent planet than
earth. Everything—the firm mountains to the left, the
spurs and undulations of the plain, the Dead Sea, the misty
heights of Jordan—is hugely dominated by the sky; even
the burnished acres of the water can reflect only a fraction of
the circumambient blue. In fact the biosphere is shallow:
space, outer space, is only an hour's drive away (space is
nearer than Jerusalem); but the Judean sky looks like infin-
ity. Below, the terrain is a terrain for war, conventional war:
conventional death, conventional wreckage, under these
same heavens. But another kind of war, a nuclear one (I
thought, with double vertigo), could wreck the *sky*. Later
that day a journalist from the *Jerusalem Post* told me about
"the Warehouse," a building in the desert surrounded by
barbed wire and armed guards, the supposed locus of Israel's
nuclear effort. It is not altogether clear—it never is—
whether Israel has the bomb or merely the ability to make

one. I want to know what use this weapon would be. What use are they, ever? Beirut and Damascus are both forty miles from Israel's border, an hour's drive away, like space. For Israel, a nuclear weapon would be a Masada weapon. That's what nuclear weapons are: Masada weapons.

Meanwhile they squat on our spiritual lives. There may be a nuclear "priesthood," but we are the supplicants, and we have no faith. The warheads are our godheads. Nuclear weapons could bring about the Book of Revelation in a matter of hours; they could do it today. Of course, no dead will rise; nothing will be revealed (*nothing* meaning two things, the absence of everything and a thing called *nothing*). Events that we call "acts of God"—floods, earthquakes, eruptions—are flesh wounds compared to the human act of nuclear war: a million Hiroshimas. Like God, nuclear weapons are free creations of the human mind. Unlike God, nuclear weapons are real. And they are here.

Revulsion at MAD is understandable and necessary. I suggest, however, that MAD is not just a political creation but a creation of the weapons themselves. Always we keep coming back to the weapons as if they were actors rather than pieces of equipment; and they earn this status, by virtue of their cosmic power. They are actors and, considered on the human scale, insane actors. The weapons are insane, they are MAD: they can assume no other form. In one of those philosopher's throat clearings, Anthony Kenny says that "weapons considered merely as inert pieces of hardware are not, of course, objects of moral evaluation. It is the uses to which they are put . . ." This isn't so. Recent evidence strongly suggests that nuclear weapons, in their inert state, are responsible for a variety of cancers and leukemias. What toxicity, what power, what range. They cause death even before they go off.

The A-bomb is a Z-bomb, and the arms race is a race between nuclear weapons and ourselves. It is them or us. What do nukes do? What are they for? Since when did we all want to kill each other? Nuclear weapons deter a nuclear holocaust by threatening a nuclear holocaust, and if things go wrong then that is what you get: a nuclear holocaust. If things don't go wrong, and continue not going wrong for the next millennium of millennia (the boasted forty years being no more than forty winks in cosmic time), you get . . . What do you get? What are we getting?

At the multiracial children's tea party the guests have, perhaps, behaved slightly better since the Keepers were introduced. Little Ivan has stopped pulling Fetnab's hair, though he is still kicking her leg under the table. Bobby has returned the slice of cake that rightfully belonged to tiny Conchita, though he has his eye on that sandwich and will probably make a lunge for it sooner or later. Out on the lawn the Keepers maintain a kind of order, but standards of behavior are pretty well as troglodytic as they ever were. At best the children seem strangely subdued or off-color. Although they are aware of the Keepers, they don't want to look at them, they don't want to catch their eye. They don't want to think about them. For the Keepers are a thousand feet tall, and covered in gelignite and razor blades, toting flamethrowers and machine guns, cleavers and skewers, and fizzing with rabies, anthrax, plague. Curiously enough, they are not looking at the children at all. With bleeding hellhound eyes, mouthing foul threats and shaking their fists, they are looking at each other. They want to take on someone their own size . . .

If they only knew it—no, if they only *believed* it—the children could simply ask the Keepers to leave. But it doesn't seem possible, does it? It seems—it seems unthinkable. A silence starts to fall across the lawn. The party has not been going for very long and must last until the end of time. Already the children are weepy and feverish. They all feel sick and want to go home.

# FIVE STORIES

# BUJAK

---

# AND THE

---

# STRONG FORCE

---

# or GOD'S DICE

---

Bujak? Yeah, I knew him. The whole street knew Bujak. I
knew him before and I knew him after. We all knew Bujak
—sixty years old, hugely slabbed and seized with muscle
and tendon, smiling at a bonfire in the yard, carrying desks
and sofas on his back, lifting a tea-chest full of books with
one hand. Bujak, the strongman. He was also a dreamer, a
reader, a babbler. . . . You slept a lot sounder knowing
that Bujak was on your street. This was 1980. I was living
in London, West London, carnival country, what the police
there call the *front line*. DR. ALIMANTADO, SONS OF THUN-
DER, RACE WAR, NO FUTURE: dry thatched dreadlocks, the
scarred girls in the steeped pubs. Those black guys, they
talked like combative drunks, all the time. If I went up to

33

Manchester to stay with my girlfriend, I always left a key with Bujak. Those hands of his, as hard as coal, the nails quite square and symmetrical, like his teeth. And the forearms, the Popeye forearms, hefty and tattoo-smudged and brutal, weapons of monstrous power. Large as he was, the energies seemed impacted in him, as though he were the essence of an even bigger man; he stood for solidity. I am as tall as Bujak, but half his weight. No, less. Bujak once told me that to create a man out of nothing would require the equivalent energy of a thousand-megaton explosion. Looking at Bujak, you could believe this. As for me, well, a single stick of TNT might do the job—a hand grenade, a firecracker. In his physical dealings with me (you know, the way someone moves across a room toward you, this can be a physical event) he showed the tender condescension that the big man shows to the small. Probably he was like that with everyone. He was protective. And then, to good Bujak, thoughtful, grinning Bujak, the worst thing happened. A personal holocaust. In the days that followed I saw and felt all of Bujak's violence.

His life went deep into the century. Warrior caste, he fought in Warsaw in 1939. He lost his father and two brothers at Katyn. He was in the resistance—all his life he was in the resistance. In that capacity he visited (and this is a story of violence, of visitation) many neat tortures on Nazi collaborators. He rose up with the Armia Kraiova and was imprisoned in December 1944. During the postwar years he worked in a touring circus, a strongman, bending bars, butting brick walls, tugging trucks with his teeth. In 1956, the year of my birth, he was there for the Polish

October, and for the November in "Hungaria." Then the United States, the halls, queues, and cubicles of Ellis Island, with wife, mother, small daughter. His wife Monika was hospitalized in New York for a minor condition; she came down with a hospital supergerm and died overnight. Bujak worked as a longshoreman in Fort Lauderdale. He took and gave many crunchy beatings—strikebreakers, mob men, union goons. But he prospered, as you're meant to do, in America. What brought him to England, I think, was a certain kind of (displaced) Polish nostalgia or snobbery, and a desire for peace. Bujak had lived the twentieth century. And then, one day, the twentieth century, a century like no other, came calling on him. Bookish Bujak himself, I'm sure, saw the calamity as in some sense postnuclear, Einsteinian. It was certainly the end of his existing universe. Yes, it was Bujak's Big Crunch.

I first met Bujak one wintry morning in the late spring of 1980—or of PN 35, if you use the postnuclear calendar that he sometimes favored. Michiko's car had something wrong with it, as usual (a flat, on this occasion), and I was down on the street grappling with the burglar tools and the spare. Compact and silent, Michiko watched me sadly. I'd managed to loosen the nuts on the collapsed wheel, but the aperture for the jack was ominously soft and sticky with rust. The long-suffering little car received the vertical spear in its chassis and stayed stoically earthbound. Now I have to say that I am already on very bad terms with the inanimate world. Even when making a cup of coffee or changing a light bulb (or a fuse!), I think—What is it with objects? Why are they so aggressive? What's their beef with *me?*

Objects and I, we can't go on like this. We must work out a compromise, a freeze, before one of us does something rash. I've got to meet with their people and hammer out a deal.

"Stop it, Sam," said Michiko.

"Get a real car," I told her.

"Please, just stop. Stop it! I'll call a towtruck or something."

"Get a real car," I said and thought—yeah, or a real boyfriend. Anyway, I was throwing the tools into their pouch, dusting my palms and wiping away my tears when I saw Bujak pacing across the road toward us. Warily I monitored his approach. I had seen this hulking Bohunk or throwback Polack from my study window, busying himself down on the street, always ready to flex his primitive can-do and know-how. I wasn't pleased to see him. I have enough of the standard-issue paranoia, or I did then. Now I've grown up a little and realize that I have absolutely nothing to fear, except the end of the world. Along with everybody else. At least in the next war there won't be any special wimps, punchbags, or unpopularity contests. Genocide has had its day and we're on to something bigger now. Suicide.

"You a Jew?" asked Bujak in his deeply speckled voice.

"Yup," I said.

"Name?"

And number? "Sam," I told him.

"Short for?"

I hesitated and felt Michi's eyes on my back.

"Is it Samuel?"

"No," I said. "Actually it's Samson."

The smile he gave told me many things, most obviously that here—here was a happy man. All eyes and teeth, the smile was ridiculous in its gaiety, its candor. But then happiness is a pretty clownish condition, when you stop to think about it. I mean, round-the-clock happiness, it's hardly an appropriate response. To me, this gave him an element of instability, of counterstrength, of violence. But Bujak here was clearly happy, in his universe. Bujak, with his happiness accessory.

"Jews usually good up here," he said, and knocked a fingertip on his shaved head. "No good with their hands."

Bujak was good with *his* hands: to prove it, he bent forward and picked up the car with them.

"You're kidding," I said. But he wasn't. As I got to work he was already shooting the breeze with Michiko, nonchalantly asking her if she'd lost any family at Nagasaki or Hiroshima. Michi had, as it happened—a cousin of her father's. This was news to me but I felt no surprise. It seems that everyone loses someone in the big deaths. Bujak changed stance freely, and, at one point, lifted a forgetful hand to scratch his skull. The car never wavered. I watched Bujak as I worked, and saw that the strength he called on owed nothing to the shoulders or the great curved back— just the arms, the arms. It was as if he were raising the lid of a cellar door, or holding up a towel while a little girl dressed on the beach. Then he roughly took the tire iron from my hands and knelt on one knee to rivet the bolts. As the grained slab of his head loomed upward again Bujak's eyes were tight and unamused, and they moved roughly too across my face. He nodded at Michi and said to me, "And who did you lose?"

"Uh?" I said. If I understood his question, then the answer was none of his business.

"I give money to Israel every year," he said. "Not much. Some. Why? Because the Polish record on the Jews is disgraceful. After the war even," he said, and grinned. "Quite disgraceful. Look. There is a tire mender in Basing Street. Tell them Bujak and they will make it for you fairly."

Thanks, we both said. Off he went, measuring the road with his strides. Later, from my study window, I saw him pruning roses in the small front garden. A little girl, his granddaughter, was crawling all over his back. I saw him often, from my study window. In those days, in 1980, I was trying to be a writer. No longer. I can't take the study life, the life of the study. This is the only story I'll ever tell, and this story is true. . . . Michiko was sold on Bujak right away and dropped a thank-you note through his door that same afternoon. But it took a while before I had really made terms with Bujak.

I asked around about this character, as you will when you're playing at writing. Like I said, everybody knew Bujak. In the streets, the pubs, the shops, they spoke of him as a fixer and handyman, omnicompetent: all the systems that keep a house going, that keep it alive—Bujak could handle them, the veins, the linings, the glands, and the bowels. He was also marked down as a definite eccentric, a stargazer, a "philosopher"—not, I gathered, a valued calling in these parts—and on occasion as an out-and-out *nutter* (one of those words that never sound right on American lips, like *quid* and *bloody*). People gave Bujak his due as a family man: once Michi and I glimpsed him quite far afield, outside the Russian church on the junction of St. Petersburg Place and Moscow Road, erect in his suit, with his mother, his daughter, and his granddaughter; I remember thinking that even huge Bujak could show the fussed delicacy you get from living in a house full of ladies. But most eagerly and vehemently, of course, they spoke of Bujak the peacekeeper, the vigilante, the rough-justice artist. They spoke of skirmishes, vendettas, one-man wars, preemptive strikes. Standing there in the pub, the shoulderless and bespectacled American with his beer mug awkwardly poised, or peering over a counter, or standing on a corner with milk carton and newspaper under my arm, I was indulged with tales of Bujak and the strong force.

The time he caught two black kids prying at a neighbor's basement window and sent them twirling into the street with two flicks of his wrist, like someone mucking out a trench. Or what he did to their big brothers when they jumped him in Golbourne Road the following night. Any brawler or burglar nabbed by Bujak soon wished himself under the hosepipe in some nice safe slammer. He took on all comers. Feuding with the council, he once dragged a skip full of rubbish a hundred yards from his front door. He went out one night and upended a truck after a row about a generator with some local building contractors. The Bujak women could walk the All Saints Road at any hour and expect no bother. And Bujak himself could silence a pub just by walking past it. He was popular, though. He was the community man, and such community as the street had devolved upon Bujak. He was our deterrent.

And it wasn't enough. . . . Now, in 1985, it is hard for me to believe that a city is anything more or other than the sum of its streets, as I sit here with the Upper West Side blatting at my window and fingering my heart. Sometimes in my dreams of New York danger I stare down over the city—and it looks half made, half wrecked, one half (the base perhaps) of something larger torn in two, frayed, twangy, moist with rain or solder. And you mean to tell me, I say to myself, that this is supposed to be a *community?* . . . My wife and daughter move around among all this, among the violations, the life-trashers, the innocent murderers. Michiko takes our little girl to the daycare center where she works. Daycare—that's good. But what about dawn care, dusk care, what about night care? If I just had a force I could enfold them with, oh, if I just had the strong force. . . . Bujak was right. In the city now there are loose components, accelerated particles—something *has* come loose, something is wriggling, lassooing, spinning toward the edge of its groove. Something must give and it isn't safe. You ought to be terribly careful. Because safety has left our lives. It's gone forever. And what do animals do when you give them only danger? They make more danger, more, much more.


It was 1980, the birth year of Solidarity, and Bujak was Polish. This combination of circumstances led me to assume that Bujak was liberal in his sentiments. Actually it didn't follow. As I proudly strolled with him to the timber yard or the home-improvement stores off the Portobello Road, Bujak would fume against the blacks, the *czarnuchy,* as they strutted and gabbled round about us. The blacks were fine, he grinningly argued, in a context of sun, surf, and plentiful bananas; but in a Western city they were just children— understandably angry children too. Once he stopped dead to marvel at two gay punks in NO FUTURE T-shirts, with hair like old ladies' bonnets, as they walked toward us hand in hand. "It's incredible, isn't it," he said, rolling the *r.* With the faggots, Bujak saw their plight, and their profusion, as an Einsteinian matter also. He confessed to the fantasy of leading a cavalry charge against the streets and their strange ensembles—the sound of the hooves, the twirling cutlasses. "A desire which I suppress of course. But if I could just press a button," he added, greedily eying the *pedaly,* the *czarnuchy,* the street dwellers as they turned and gesticulated and reshuffled and moved on.

Violence in a man is usually the overspill of something else. You know how it is. You see these guys. I appear to have an almost disabling sensitivity to violence in other men, a fallout detector for those spots of waste or exorbitance that spill over into force. Like a canary in a prewar coalmine, I check out early when there is violence, when there is poison in the air. What is this propensity? Call it *fear,* if you like. *Fear* will do fine. The raised voice in the restaurant and its sour tang of brutality and booze, the look a man will give his wife which demotes her on the human scale, which prepares her for the human disgrace of violence, the pumping leg, the fizzing eye, the public bar at ten fifty-five. I see all this—my body sees it, and gives me adrenaline, gives me sweat. I faint at the sight of blood. I faint at the sight of a Band-Aid, an aspirin. This sense of critical fragility (myself, my wife, my daughter, even the poor planet, baby blue in its shawls), it drove me from my study in the end. The study life is all thought and anxiety and I cannot take the study life anymore.

Late at night, over at Bujak's large, aromatic, icon-infested apartment (the blue glow of saints, candles, vigils), I scanned the big Pole for the excrescences of violence. His mother, old Roża, made the tea. The old woman ("rouge" with an *a* on the end), she calmed me with her iconic presence, the moist hair grained like silver, as Bujak talked about the strong force, the energy locked in matter. Grinning in the gloom, Bujak told me what he had done to the Nazi collaborator in Warsaw, in 1943. Boy, I thought; I bet the guy didn't do much collaborating after that. However, I couldn't conceal my distaste. "But aren't you glad?" urged Bujak. No, I said, why should I be? "You lost two grandparents to these people." Yeah, I said. So? That doesn't change anything. "Revenge," said Bujak simply. Revenge is overrated, I told him. And out of date. He looked at me with violent contempt. He opened his hands in an explanatory gesture: the hands, the arms, the policemen of his will. Bujak was a big fan of revenge. He had a lot of time for revenge.

I once saw him use those hands, those arms. I saw it all from my study window, the four-paneled screen (moon-spotted, with refracting crossbar) through which the world

came in at me then. I saw the four guys climb from the two
cars and steady themselves in front of Bujak's stoop. Did I
hear a scream from within, a cry of warning or yearning?
. . . Bujak's daughter gave the old man a lot of grief. Her
first name was Leokadia. Her second name was trouble.
Rural-looking yet glamorous, thirty-three, tall, plump,
fierce, and tearful, she was the unstable element in Bujak's
nucleus. She had, I noticed, two voices, one for truth, and
one for nonsense, one for lies. Against the brown and shiny
surface of her old-style dresses, the convex and the concave
were interestingly disposed. *Her* daughter, little Boguslawa, was the byblow of some chaotic twelve-hour romance.
It was well known on the street that Leokadia had round
heels: the sort of girl (we used to say) who went into a hot
flush every time she saw an army personnel carrier. She even
made a pitch at me, here at the flat one time. Needless to
say, I failed to come across. I had my reasons: fear of reprisals
from Michiko and Bujak himself (they both loomed in my
mind, incongruously equal in size); also, more basically,
I'm by no means sure I could handle someone like Leokadia
in the cot. All that breast and haunch. All those freckles
and tears. . . . For six months she had been living with a
man who beat her, lithe little Pat, sinewy, angular, wired
very tight. I think she beat him too, a bit. But violence is
finally a masculine accomplishment. Violence—now that's
man's work. Leokadia kept going back to Pat, don't ask me
why. I don't know. They don't know. There she goes again,
ticking back to him on her heels, with black eye, grazed
cheek, wrenched hair. Nobody knows why. Not even they
know. Bujak, surprisingly, stayed out of it, held his dis-

tance, remained solid—though he did try to keep the little girl, Boguslawa, safely at home, out of the turbulence. You would often see old Roża ferrying the kid from one flat to the other. After her second spell in the hospital (cracked ribs this time) Leokadia called it a day and went home for good. Then Pat showed up with his pals and found Bujak waiting.

The three men (I saw it all) had an unmistakable look about them, with that English bad-boy build, proud guts and tapering legs that bent backward from the knee down, sparse-haired with old-young faces, as if they had done their aging a lot quicker than one year at a time. I don't know whether these guys would have frightened anybody much on the American circuit, but I guess they were big enough and their intention was plain. (Did you read about the Yablonsky murders? In the States these days, if you're on the list, they come in and do the whole family. Yes, they just nuke you now.) Anyway, they frightened me. I sat writhing at my desk as Pat led them through the garden gate. I hated the flares of his jeans, the compact running shoes, the tight Fred Perry. Then the front door opened: bespectacled Bujak, wearing braces over his vest, old, huge. In a reflex that spelt seriousness and scorn, the men loosened their shoulders and let their hands dangle in readiness. Words were exchanged—demand, denial. They moved forward.

Now I must have blinked, or shut my eyes, or ducked (or fainted). I heard three blows on a regular second beat, clean, direct, and atrocious, each one like an ax splitting frozen wood. When I looked up, Pat and one of his friends were lying on the steps; the other guys were backing away, backing away from the site of this incident, this demonstration. Expressionlessly Bujak knelt to do something extra to Pat on the floor. As I watched, he tugged back the hair and carefully poked a neutronium fist into Pat's upturned face. I had to go and lie down after that. But a couple of weeks later I saw Pat sitting alone in the London Apprentice; he was shivering remorsefully in the corner behind the jukebox; the pleated welt on his cheek bore all the colors of flame, and he was drinking his beer through a straw. In that one blow he had taken payment for everything he had given Leokadia.

With Bujak, I was always edging into friendship. I don't know if I ever really made it. Differences of age aren't easy. Differences of strength aren't easy. Friendship isn't easy. When Bujak's own holocaust came calling, I was some help to him; I was better than nothing. I went to the court. I went to the cemetery. I took my share of the strong force, what little I could take. . . . Perhaps a dozen times during that summer, before the catastrophe came (it was heading toward him slowly, gathering speed), I sat up late on his back porch when all the women had gone to bed. Bujak stargazed. He talked and drank his tea. "Traveling at the speed of light," he said one time, "you could cross the whole universe in less than a second. Time and distance would be annihilated, and all futures possible." No shit? I thought. Or again: "If you could linger on the brink of a singularity, time would be so slow that a night would pass in forty-five seconds, and there would be three American elections in the space of seven days." Three American elections, I said to myself. Whew, what a boring week. And why is *he* the dreamer, while I am bound to the low earth? Feeling mean, I often despised the dreaming Bujak, but I entertained late-night warmth for him too, for the accretions of experience (time having worked on his face like a sculptor, awful slow), and I feared him—I feared the energy coiled, seized, and locked in Bujak. Staring up at our little disk of stars (and perhaps there are better residential galaxies than our own: cleaner, safer, more gentrified), I sensed only the false still-ness of the black nightmap, its beauty concealing great and routine violence, the fleeing universe, with matter racing apart, exploding to the limits of space and time, all tugs and curves, all hubble and doppler, infinitely and eternally hostile. . . . This evening, as I write, the New York sky is also full of stars—the same stars. There. There is Michiko coming down the street, hand in hand with our little girl. They made it. Home at last. Above them the gods shoot crap with their black dice: threes and fives and ones. The Plough has just rolled a four and a two. But who throws the six, the six, the six?

All peculiarly modern ills, all fresh distortions and dis-tempers, Bujak attributed to one thing: Einsteinian knowl-edge, knowledge of the strong force. It was his central paradox that the greatest—the purest, the most magical—genius of our time should have introduced the earth to such squalor, profanity, and panic. "But how very like the twen-tieth century," he said: this was always going to be the age when irony really came into its own. I have cousins and uncles who speak of Einstein as if he were some hero ball-player captaining a team called the Jews ("the mind on him," "look at the mind on the guy"). Bujak spoke of Einstein as if he were God's literary critic, God being a poet. I, more stolidly, tend to suspect that God is a novelist —a garrulous and deeply unwholesome one too. . . . Actually Bujak's theory had a lot of appeal for me. It was, at least, holistic. It answered the big question. You know the question I mean, and its cumulative disquiet, its compound interest. You ask yourself the question every time you open a newspaper or switch on the TV or walk the streets among sons of thunder. New formations, deformations. You know the question. It reads: *Just what the hell is going on around here?*

The world looks worse every day. Is it worse, or does it just look it? The world gets older. The world has seen and done it all. Boy, is it beat. It's suicidal. Like Leokadia, the world has done too many things too many times with too many people, done it this way, that way, with him, with him. The world has been to so many parties, been in so many fights, lost its keys, had its handbag stolen, drunk too much. It all adds up. A tab is presented. Our ironic destiny. Look at the modern infamies, the twentieth-century sins. Some are strange, some banal, but they all offend the eye, covered in their newborn vernix. Gratuitous or recreational crimes of violence, the ever-less-tacit totalitarianism of money (money—what *is* this shit anyway?), the pornographic proliferation, the nuclear collapse of the family (with the breeders all going critical, and now the children running too), the sappings and distortions of a mediated reality, the sexual abuse of the very old and the very young (of the weak, the weak): what is the hidden denominator here, and what could explain it *all?*

To paraphrase Bujak, as I understood him. We live in a shameful shadowland. Quietly, our idea of human life has changed, thinned out. We can't help but think less of it now. The human race has declassed itself. It does not live anymore; it just survives, like an animal. We endure the suicide's shame, the shame of the murderer, the shame of the victim. Death is all we have in common. And what does that do to life? Such, at any rate, was Bujak's damage check. If the world disarmed tomorrow, he believed, the species would still need at least a century of recuperation, after its entanglement, its flirtation, after its thing with the strong force.

Academic in any case, since Bujak was insuperably convinced that the end was on its way. How could man (that dangerous creature—I mean, look at his *record*), how could man resist the intoxication of the Perfect Crime, one that destroys all evidence, all redress, all pasts, all futures? I was enough of a peacenik, optimist, and funker to take the other view. A dedicated follower of fear, I always thought that the fat brute and the big bastard would maintain their standoff: they know that if one fist is raised then the whole pub comes down anyway. Not a masterpiece of reassurance, I agree—not at ten fifty-five on a Saturday night, with the drink still coming.

"Deterrence theory," said Bujak, with his grin. "It's not just a bad theory. It's not even a theory. It's an insanity."

"That's why you have to go further."

"You are a unilateralist?"

"Well yeah," I said. "Someone's got to make a start sometime. Make a start. England is historically well placed to give it a try. So the Russians take Europe, maybe. But that risk must be smaller than the other risk, which is infinite."

"This changes nothing. The risk is unaltered. All you do here is make life easier to part with."

"Well, I just think you have to make a start."

Our arguments always ended on the same side street. I maintained that the victim of a first strike would have no reason to retaliate, and would probably not do so.

"Oh?" said Bujak.

"What would be the point? You'd have nothing to protect. No country, no people. You'd gain nothing. Why add to it all?"

"Revenge."

"Oh yeah. The heat of the battle. But that's not a *reason*."

"In war, revenge is a reason. Revenge is as reasonable as anything. They say nuclear war will not be really *war* but something else. True, but it will feel like war to those who fight it."

On the other hand, he added, nobody could guess how people would react under the strong force. Having crossed that line the whole world would be crazy or animal and certainly no longer human.

One day in the fall of 1980 Bujak traveled north. I never knew why. I saw him on the street that morning, a formidable sight in the edifice of his dark blue suit. Something about his air of courtly gaiety, his cap, his tie, suggested to me that he was off to investigate an old ladyfriend. The sky was gray and gristly, with interesting bruises, the street damp and stickered with leaves. Bujak pointed a tight umbrella at his own front door. "I come back tomorrow night," he said. "Keep an eye on them."

"Me? Well, sure. Okay."

"Leokadia, I learn, is pregnant. Two months. Pat. Oh, Pat—he really was too bad." Then he shrugged powerfully and said, "But I'm pleased. Look at Boguslawa. Her father was an animal too. But look at her. A flower. An angel from heaven."

And off he went, pacing out the street, content, if necessary, to walk the whole way. That afternoon I looked in on the girls and drank a cup of tea with old Roża. Christ, I remember thinking, what is it with these Polacks? Roża was seventy-eight. By that age *my* mother had been dead for twenty years. (Cancer. Cancer is the *other* thing—the third thing. Cancer will come for me too, I guess. Sometimes I feel it right in front of me, fizzing like television inches from my face.) I sat there and wondered how the quality of wildness was distributed among the Bujak ladies. With pious eyes and hair like antique silver, Roża was nonetheless the sort of old woman who still enjoyed laughing at the odd salacious joke—and she laughed very musically, one hand raised in gentle propitiation. "Hey, Roża," I would say: "I got one for you." And she would start laughing before I began. Little Boguslawa—seven, silent, sensitive—lay reading by the fire, her eyes lit by the page. Even the brawny beauty Leokadia seemed steadier, her eyes more easily containing their glow. She spoke to me now as levelly as she used to before we had that awkward tangle in my apartment. You know, I think the reason she put out for the boys so much was the usual thing about trying to accumulate approval. Approval is funny stuff, and some people need a lot more of it than others. Also she was obviously very rich in her female properties and essences; being prudent isn't so easy for girls kitted out like that. Now she sat there equably doing nothing. The red flag was down. All was calm with her dangerous floods and tides. A moony peace—Michi was like that herself sometimes, when our child was on the way. Our little one. Expecting. I stuck around for an hour or so and then crossed the road again, back to my study and its small life. I sat and read *Mosby's Memoirs* for the rest of the evening; and through my window I did indeed keep an eye on the Bujak front door. The next day was Friday. I looked in on the ladies to drop off a key before heading north myself —to Manchester and to Michiko. Meanwhile, energetic actors, vivid representatives of the twentieth century—Einstein's monsters—were on their way south.

At midnight on Saturday Bujak returned. All I know about what he found I got from the newspapers and the police, together with a couple of stray details that Bujak let slip. In any event I will add nothing; I will add nothing to what Bujak found. . . . He had no premonition until he placed his key in the lock and saw that the door was open and gave softly to his touch. He proceeded in deep silence. The hall had an odd smell to it, the smell of cigarette smoke and jam. Bujak tipped open the living-room door. The room looked like half of something torn in two. On the floor an empty vodka bottle seemed to tip slightly on its axis. Leokadia lay naked in the corner. One leg was bent at an impossible angle. Bujak moved through the terrible rooms. Roza and Boguslawa lay on their beds, naked, contorted, frozen, like Leokadia. In Leokadia's room two strange men were sleeping. Bujak closed the bedroom door behind him and removed his cap. He came closer. He leaned forward to seize them. Just before he did so he flexed his arms and felt the rustle of the strong force.


This happened five years ago. Yes, I'm here to tell you that the world is still around, in 1985. We live in New York now. I teach. The students come to me, and then they leave. There are gaps, spaces in between things big enough for me to glimpse the study life and know again that I can't take it. My daughter is four years old. I was present at the birth, or I tried to be. First I was sick; then I hid; then I fainted. Yeah, I did real good. Found and revived, I was led back to the delivery room. They placed the blood-fringed bundle in my arms. I thought then and I think now: How will the poor little bitch make it? How will she *make* it? But I'm learning to live with her, with the worry bomb, the love bomb. Last summer we took her to England. The pound was weak and the dollar was strong—the bold, the swaggering dollar, plunderer of Europe. We took her to London, London West, carnival country with its sons of thunder.

Bujak country. I'd called my landlady and established that
Bujak, too, was still around, in 1984. There was a question
I needed to ask him. And Michi and I wanted to show Bujak
our girl, little Roża, named for the old woman.


It was old Roża whom I had thought of most fixedly, during
the worst car journey of my life, as we drove from Manchester to London, from fair weather into foul, into Sunday
weather. That morning, over coffee and yogurt in her cubicle, Michi handed me the smudged and mangling tabloid.
"Sam?" she said. I stared at the story, at the name, and
realized that the rat life is not somewhere else anymore, is
not on the other side but touches your life, my life. . . .
Cars are terrible things and no wonder Bujak hated them.
Cars are cruel creatures, vicious bastards, pitiless and inex-
orable, with only this one idea, this A-to-B-idea. They
made no allowances. Down we slid through the motorway
wheel-squirt. Neighbors gathered as we parked, the men
bearing umbrellas, the women with their arms folded, shaking their heads. I crossed the street and rang the bell. And
again. And for what? I tried the back door, the kitchen
porch. Then Michiko called me. Together we stared
through the living-room window. Bujak sat at the table,
hunched forward as if he needed all the power of his back
and shoulders just to hold position, just to keep his rest
energy seized, skewered. Several times I knocked on the
glass. He never moved. There was a noise in my ear and
the seconds fussed and fussed, slower than a fuse. The street
felt like a cave. I turned to Michi and her four-lidded eyes.

We stood and watched each other through the heavy rain.

Later, I was some help to him, I think, when it was my turn to tangle with the strong force. For some reason Michiko could bear none of this; the very next day she bowed out on me and went straight back to America. Why? She had and still has ten times my strength. Perhaps that was it. Perhaps she was too strong to bend to the strong force. Anyway, I make no special claims here. . . . In the evenings Bujak would come and sit in my kitchen, filling the room. He wanted proximity, he wanted to be elsewhere. He didn't talk. The small corridor hummed with strange emanations, pulsings, fallout. It was often hard to move, hard to breathe. What do strong men feel when their strength is leaving them? Do they listen to the past or do they just hear things—voices, music, the cauldron bubble of distant hooves? I'll be honest and say what I thought. I thought, Maybe he'll have to kill me, not because he wants to or wishes me harm, but because he has taken so much harm himself. This would free him of it, for a while. Something had to give. I endured the aftermath, the radiation. That was the only thing I had to contribute.

Also I went with him to court, and was at his side throughout *that* injury, that serial injury. The two defendants were Scotsmen, bail beaters from Dundee, twentyish, wanted—not that it made much difference who they were. There was no plea of insanity, nor indeed any clear sign of it. Sanity didn't enter into the thing. You couldn't understand anything they said so a policeman translated. Their story went like this. Having had more pints of beer than

were perhaps strictly good for them, the two men took up
with Leokadia Bujak on the street and offered to walk her
home. Asked inside, they in turn made passionate love to
the young woman, at her invitation, and then settled down
for a refreshing nap. While they slept, some other party had
come in and done all these terrible things. Throughout
Bujak sat there, quietly creaking. He and I both knew
that Leokadia might have done something of the kind,
on another night, in another life, Christ, she might have
done—but with these dogs, these superdogs, underdogs,
threadbare rodents with their orange teeth? It didn't matter
anyway. Who *cared*. Bujak gave his evidence. The jury was
out for less than twenty minutes. Both men got eighteen
years. From my point of view, of course (for me it was the
only imponderable), the main question was never asked, let
alone answered: it had to do with those strange seconds in
Leokadia's bedroom, Bujak alone with the two men. Nobody asked the question. I would ask it, four years later. I
couldn't ask it then. . . . The day after sentencing I had a
kind of a breakdown. With raw throat and eyes and nose
streaming I hauled myself onto a jet. I didn't even dare say
good-by. At Kennedy what do I find but Michiko staring
me in the face and telling me she's pregnant. There and
then I went down on my lousy knees and begged her not to
have it. But she had it all right—two months early. Jesus,
a new horror story by Edgar Allan Poe: The Premature
Baby. Under the jar, under the lamp, jaundice, pneumonia
—she even had a heart attack. So did I, when they told me.
She made it in the end, though. She's great now, in 1985.
You should see her. It is the love bomb and its fallout that

energize you in the end. You couldn't begin to do it without
the love. . . . That's them on the stairs, I think. Yes, in
they come, changing everything. Here is Roża, and here is
Michiko, and here am I.


Bujak was still on the street. He had moved, from 45 to 84,
but he was still on the street. We asked around. The whole
street knew Bujak. And there he was in the front garden,
watching a fire as it flexed and cracked, the snakeheads of
flame taking sudden bites from the air—snakes of fire, in
the knowledge garden. After all, we coped with fire, when
it came; we didn't all get broiled and scorched. He looked
up. The ogre's smile hadn't changed that much, I thought,
although the presence of the man was palpably reduced.
Still old and huge in his vest, but the mass, the holding
energy softened and dispersed. Well, something had to
give. Bujak had adopted or been adopted by or at any rate
made himself necessary to a large and assorted household,
mostly Irish. The rooms were scrubbed, bare, vigorous, and
orderly, with all that can-do can do. There was lunch on the
sun-absorbing pine table: beer, cider, noise, and the sun's
phototherapy. The violence with which the fiftyish redhead
scolded Bujak about his appearance made it plain to me that
there was a romantic attachment. Even then, with the old
guy nearer seventy than sixty, I thought with awe of Bujak
in the sack. Bujak in the bag! Incredibly, his happiness was
intact—unimpaired, entire. How come? Because, I think,
his generosity extended not just to the earth but to the
universe—or simply that he loved all matter, its spin and
charm, redshifts and blueshifts, its underthings. The hap-

piness was there. It was the strength that had gone from him forever. Over lunch he said that, a week or two ago, he had seen a man hitting a woman on the street. He shouted at them and broke it up. Physically, though, he was powerless to intercede—*helpless,* he said, with a shrug. Actually you could feel the difference in the way he moved, in the way he crossed the room toward you. The strength had gone, or the will to use it.

Afterward he and I stepped out onto the street. Michiko had ducked out of this last encounter, choosing instead to linger with the ladies. But we had the girl with us, little Roża, asleep on Bujak's shoulder. I watched him without fear. He wouldn't drop the folded child. He had taken possession of Roża with his arms.

As if by arrangement we paused at number 45. Black kids now played in the garden with a winded red football. Things were falling away between Bujak and me, and suddenly it seemed that you could say what you liked. So I said, "Adam. No offense. But why didn't you kill them? *I* would have. I mean, if I think of Michi and Roża . . ." But in fact you cannot think it, you cannot go near it. The thought is fire. "Why didn't you kill the sons of bitches? What stopped you?"

"Why?" he asked, and grinned. "What would have been the reason?"

"Come on. You could have done it, easy. Self-defense. No court on earth would have sent you down."

"True. It occurred to me."

"Then what happened? Did you—did you feel too weak all of a sudden? Did you just feel too weak?"

"On the contrary. When I had their heads in my hands I

thought how incredibly easy to grind their faces together—
until they drowned in each other's faces. But no."

But no. Bujak had simply dragged the men by the arms
(half a mile, to the police station in Harrow Road), like a
father with two frantic children. He delivered them and
dusted his hands.

"Christ, they'll be out in a few years. Why *not* kill them?
Why not?"

"I had no wish to add to what I found. I thought of my
dead wife Monika. I thought—they're all dead now. I
couldn't add to what I saw there. Really the hardest thing
was to touch them at all. You know the wet tails of rats?
Snakes? Because I saw that they weren't human beings at
all. They had no idea what human life was. No idea! Terrible mutations, a disgrace to their human molding. An eternal disgrace. If I had killed them then I would still be
strong. But you must start somewhere. You must make a
start."

And now that Bujak has laid down his arms, I don't know
why, but I am minutely stronger. I don't know why—I
can't tell you why.

He once said to me: "There must be more matter in the
universe than we think. Else the distances are horrible. I'm
nauseated." Einsteinian to the end, Bujak was an Oscilla-
tionist, claiming that the Big Bang will forever alternate
with the Big Crunch, that the universe would expand only
until unanimous gravity called it back to start again. At
that moment, with the cosmos turning on its hinges, light
would begin to travel backward, received by the stars and
pouring from our human eyes. If, and I can't believe it, time

would also be reversed, as Bujak maintained (will we move backward too? Will we have any say in things?), then this moment as I shake his hand shall be the start of my story, his story, our story, and we will slip downtime of each other's lives, to meet four years from now, when, out of the fiercest grief, Bujak's lost women will reappear, born in blood (and we will have our conversations, too, backing away from the same conclusion), until Boguslawa folds into Leokadia, and Leokadia folds into Monika, and Monika is there to be enfolded by Bujak until it is her turn to recede, kissing her fingertips, backing away over the fields to the distant girl with no time for him (will that be any easier to bear than the other way around?), and then big Bujak shrinks, becoming the weakest thing there is, helpless, indefensible, naked, weeping, blind and tiny, and folding into Roza.

# INSIGHT AT

# FLAME LAKE

*Ned's Diary*

*July 16.* Well it certainly is a pleasure to have Dan come and summer with us up here at Flame Lake. I'm glad to do it. We have him till mid-August. There'll be problems—Fran and I agree on this—but right now he seems manageable enough, though heavily haunted. Fran's a little upset too, of course, but we talked it through, the night before Dan came, and straightened the whole thing out. I spoke on the phone with Dr. Slizard, who warned me that the extra medication that Dan's taking would make him sullen and unresponsive for the first three or four days. And he is grieving. Poor Dan—I feel for the kid. So brilliant, and so troubled, like his father, God rest his soul. I am grieving too. Even though we weren't that close (he was old enough to be my father), still, when your brother goes, it's like a little death. It's a hell of a thing. Dan hides from the heat. He keeps to his room. Dr. Slizard told me to expect this. I'm hoping the baby will amuse and distract him. Fran is nervous about that also, however. All right. It won't be the carefree summer we were planning on. But we'll work it out. And surely the light and space of Flame Lake will be useful therapy for Dan and may even help to ease his problem.

### Dan's Notebook

The lake is like an explosion. . . .

Dr. Slizard, in our long discussion after Dad's death, assured me that I have *insight* into my condition. I have *insight:* I know I'm sick. In a sense this was news to me— but then, how could you feel like I feel and not know something was up? Yet there are people with my condition who do *not* have *insight.* They feel like I feel and they think it's cool. Dad had no *insight.*

For the time being, with the extra medication and every- thing, I keep to my room. Calmly I note the usual side reactions: sudden tightening of the tongue, unprompted blushing, drags of nausea, beaked headaches. All food tastes the same. It tastes of nothing, of dryness and nothing. There is the expected *loss of affect*—though I can see, with my *insight,* that it is more pronounced than ever before. Not yet ready for the heat, I sit in my room and listen to the helpless weeping of the baby. The baby seems cute enough. All babies are cute enough: they have to be, evolutionarily speaking. Her name, they tell me, is Harriet, or *Hattie.*

I'm grateful to Uncle Ned and, I guess, to his new wife
Francesca. She is young, plump, and deeply dark. I know
it's ninety degrees out there but she really ought to wear
more clothes. In certain lights she has a soft mustache. She
is small but she is big: four-feet-eleven in all directions.
She's like a baby herself. I have read widely on the subject
of schizophrenia. Or, if you prefer, I have read narrowly but
with intensity. I have read Dr. Slizard's influential mono-
graph, *Schizophrenia,* forty or fifty times. I never leave home
without it. Slizard doesn't say much about schizophrenic
sexuality because, apparently, there isn't that much to say.
It's not a hot scene, schizophrenia. Hardly anybody gets
laid.

Behind the comfortable shacklike house there is a forest
where, tomorrow, I may go walking. For the time being
the forest looks too callow and self-conscious. The greenery
is so green. So wooden is the wood. With its glitter-sizzle
and the proton play of the waterskaters on its surface, the
lake—the lake is like an explosion, in the last split second
before it explodes.

## Ned's Diary

*July 19.* Although Dan is no problem and continues to be
quite manageable, I have to say that, on occasion, he comes
close to straining our patience. But that's all right. Patience
is an activity, not a state. You can't just expect to *be* patient.
You work at it. You beef it up. Mealtimes is when we seem
to need our patience most. We need all the patience we can
get. Poor Dan, he has difficulty eating. His mouth appears
to be painfully dry. He chews slowly, and forever. There is

a kind of leaden suspense over the table as we wait for the disappearance of each epic mouthful. Give him a slice of vividly juicy cantaloupe and it turns to bark between his jaws. Fran and I find ourselves lurching into the craziest conversations—we talk about *anything*—just to cover for the kid. And despite his extra medication, his grief pills, Dan is no zombie. I sometimes wish he was, but he's not. He knows. His blushes are really something to see. This morning I called Dr. Slizard at the Section. He said that Dan is sure to improve in a couple of days and will start to communicate. Fran worries about the way Dan looks at the baby. My anxiety about Harriet is more general. If you can believe—or absorb—what you read in the newspapers, it is apparently open season on babies and children. People seem to have gotten the idea suddenly that they can do what they like with them. She's safe here of course, but then there's the crib-death gimmick, dreamed up to ensure that parents get no peace of mind *at all*. Every morning when I hear Hattie crying or babbling I think—Great. She made it. Fran worries about the way Dan looks at the baby. I tell her he looks at everything that way—at me, at the walls, at the dragonflies, at Flame Lake.

### Dan's Notebook

Days are hot and endless.

The fish do their fish thing. They swim with their shimmy, then rise to gulp the waiting bugs. The bugs oblige: they go along with the deal. Ned does his Ned thing, and so does Fran. As for the baby, as for *Hattie,* well, I withhold judgment for the time being.

Last night I made a distinguished addition to my vast repertoire of atomic dreams, my dreams of nuclear supercatastrophe (you could hardly call them *nightmares* anymore). The last civilian is running across the last plain pursued by the last pilot in the last aircraft with the last warhead. These last two actors are moving at the same speed—an interesting departure from the usual crux (escape, weird retardation), with the aircraft experiencing all the human metal fatigue of nightmare. The last civilian runs with a ragged and desperate stride. The last pilot stalks him heavily through the smoke. I cannot tell whether I am the last civilian or the last pilot or simply the last observer, and it doesn't matter, because all will vanish in the last flash-boom and glitter-sizzle, in the last pouring insult of light.

Uncle Ned was twenty years younger than my father. On the other hand, he is twenty years older than Francesca, this new wife of his. She watches television for hours, or at least she is present while it's on. She reads the dumb stories in the dumb magazines: how Elizabeth Taylor licked her drink problem; how Cher's house is seriously haunted; how President Kennedy is alive and well, living with Buddy Holly on the planet Krypton. Fran sprawls with the baby and listens to rock-pop all day long. That *music*—its fatuous lack of complication: songs of personal growth. With all that brown flesh of hers Francesca takes up a lot of space. She is prodigious. She floods the room. It goes without saying that Ned cannot satisfy her. She has one baby, but she will soon be wanting more.

Like most schizophrenics, I was born in the winter quarter. Many people are baffled by this seasonal disposition.

With *insight,* however, the explanation seems straightforward enough. Fall and winter are the hardest times for the schizophrenic. They feel terribly schizophrenic in the fall and winter. Not until March or April do they feel like making love. Not until March or April do they feel like making schizophrenic babies.

Dad was a fat schizophrenic. I am a thin one, so far. He had plenty of *buffer tissue* and could function normally—indeed brilliantly—for long periods. His psychotic breaks were few and far between. But the last break broke him. Suicide. I never consider suicide. I never do. I never even think about it. It just isn't an option. Dad was a physicist, of a kind. I'm going to be one too. He worked in the subatomic realm. I am attracted to radio and x-ray astronomy, to cosmology and uranometry—to the stars. I can see them now, as I sit in the screened porch and write these words: the heavenly bodies, so gravely, so heavily, so forbiddingly embroidered onto the fabric of space-time.

I can sit outside now, in the black shade, often for an hour at a stretch. It is like breathing fire. The baby Harriet, wearing only a diaper, flaps about on the ground among the twigs and bits of bark, the needled carpet of pine. Occasionally the baby pauses in its baby projects and together we squint out at the lake's heavy water and listen to the background radiation of the insects in the encircling forest.

### Ned's Diary

*July 22.* Well now—progress, distinct improvements! We have a way to go yet, of course. I wouldn't call him happy-go-lucky exactly, but at least he looks a lot less like Franz

Kafka or Ivan Lendl (yes, Lendl, two sets down to his worst enemy and trailing love-five in the third). He goes outside, he doodles in his notebook, he has some color in those long cheeks. To smile as you take your chair at the table is not the task it was a few days ago. Fran is far more relaxed, though a little faint, as we all are, with the temperatures we're experiencing (the baby stares at all this heat around her as if she won't ever believe it). We no longer feel, for instance, that we need to hide out in our bedroom. Sure, there are still weird things. The kid is covered with mosquito bites. He looks as though he has measles. They seem to go for him in a big way, because none of us are troubled by them. One time I walked past him on the lakefront and there were five or six of the little bastards patiently feeding on his face. Fran remarked that Dan has an odor, not unpleasant exactly, like bruised fruit (his father had it too, sometimes), and maybe that's what attracts the bugs. I asked him if he wanted some repellent or anything but he just smiled and said—It's okay, Uncle Ned, it's no big thing, I'll avoid them now. You see, he's so numbed up on all the pills and chemicals he takes, he doesn't feel the bites. He feels no pain. . . . He seems to be delighted by Harriet, as indeed we all are. Maybe Hattie swung it for him. I have to say that she is just the dream baby. Coming to parenthood late in life—well, I count my blessings. A while ago I had nothing. Now here are these two little honeys. Parental love is strange, and so fearful. I love Fran for her qualities. I love Hattie for her life. I don't want anything from her, except her life. I just want her to be. I would die for that. I just want her to be.

*Dan's Notebook*

No, I don't think I've ever felt calmer.

It was a simple and courageous move: yesterday I ceased all medication, not only the sedatives but the megavitamins —and the antipsychotics. Slizard would be mad if he knew. But Slizard will never know. I am deprogramming myself, once and for all. From now on I will rely exclusively on *insight*. Already I can feel the symptoms pressing in on me, looking for an opening, seeking me out. Some are really rather bizarre, or they would be, if I had less *insight*.

Let me give an example. This afternoon I was lying on the living-room floor, watching the way the overhead fan deranged the rafter cobwebs (and I am surrounded here, you understand, by the usual furniture of lakeside life, with its shanty feel, the damp salt, the fishing tackle, the graphs of the screens charted by the corpses of bugs). Heralded by the familiar double shuffle, the sound of handsteps, kneesteps, little Harriet crawled in from the kitchen. She paused. I turned my head. The baby gave a smile of greedy recognition, and I guess she was about fifteen feet away when, "before my eyes," she started to grow. Within a second she was as large as a five-year-old; within a second more she was the size of a pig. I lay there as she billowed like a circus fat lady, the face growing faster than the body until it filled the room, my whole vision, until it seemed to burst the bounds of the house itself. Alarming? Not really. A routine case of *size-constancy breakdown*. All the baby had done was crawl toward me. Our noses were almost touching, and I had a fisheye-lens view of her marbled eyes, her food-storing

cheeks, her depthless teeth, and the ears, translucent, glow-
ing like eyelids shut to the sun.

Dad was one of the fathers of the nuclear age. Then, when
the thing was born, he became its son, along with everybody
else. So Dad really threw an odd curve on that whole deal
about fathers and sons. First he was the thing's father, then
he was the thing's son. Great distortions and malformations
should clearly be expected to follow on from such a reversal.

He worked in delivery systems, bus-and-warhead tech-
nologies, Multiple Independent Reentry Vehicles—the
MIRVs. My urine contains bufotenine, a chemical originally
isolated from toad venom. Bufotenine shows mauve in certain tests. When I am hallucinating, there is more bufotenine, more mauve, in my urine than when I don't. Tonight I
will pour all my pills into Flame Lake, and go it alone.
Tomorrow, perhaps, now that Fran has stopped dragging
Uncle Ned off to their room the whole time for sex, I will
tell them the truth about the baby. I will break it to them
about the baby. Meanwhile I stare into the brilliance and
burnish, into the mauve of the MIRVed lake.

### Ned's Diary

*July 24.* No break in the weather. Dan continues to come
on wonderfully well. He has bouts of agitation and gloom
—but who doesn't? No, he's much, much happier. Those
chance meetings you have twenty times a day in a shared
house are no longer a matter of courteous disquiet. I'm
pleased to see the kid, and he's pleased to see me. We've
put the baby back in her room, next to Dan's. She's a
powerful little sleeper (twelve hours a night, plus naps!),

and when she does wake in the small hours she just babbles to herself for a while and then checks out again. It doesn't bother Dan. But the heat does. Instead of getting cooler it just gets hotter. Someone has his thumb on the controls. Fran handles it with cold baths and about fifteen dips a day. Otherwise she schlepps around in that youthful world of TV, radio, and photoprint. Actually I'm touched by her appetite for all that garbage. What the hell. Even the *Trib* reads like a shock-sheet these days. Maybe the whole world is just turning to trash. Dan won't go in the water. He sits under the fan. I can talk to him now about his problem— the problem he has when relating to reality. And at last I have the freedom to address all *my* reality problems, the pump, the roof, the cesspit, the loose screens, that wreck of a jeep (I think I'll take the plates off and use it as a tractor). I had Dan help me shift the logs from the turkey hut to the storeroom. He ran back and forth all afternoon and stacked wood till his fingers bled.

### Dan's Notebook

In all probability Fran senses that I am still a virgin.

How else am I supposed to explain her behavior? She swims bare-ass in the excited lake, and makes sure I am watching. I have strolled into the bathroom and seen her lying there in her birthday suit: for a while she pretends not to notice; then she asks me to leave but makes no move to cover herself. Her heavy flesh shines a deeper brown in the moisture. She breastfeeds the baby right in front of my nose.

Francesca has obviously taken it upon herself to initiate

me into the so-called mysteries of sexual praxis. She goes to bed deliberately early, and Uncle Ned is soon obliged to follow. Most nights they make love in absolute silence (presumably she insists on this, to keep me guessing), but once, as I knelt there outside their room, she lost control and openly sought me out with her cries of pain and yearning. All these complications will make it much harder for me to break the truth to her about the baby.

Down at the Section, Dad had a Russian friend, a defector and a staunch American, though he often moaned and wept —and sang—about his beloved motherland when he'd taken a drink or two. (Everybody drinks up a storm, down at the Section; and Slizard heads a big team.) Whenever they said good-by, in person or on the telephone, they always signed off in the same way. Dad: "Death to the babies." Andrei: "And to your babies." Dad: "And to your babies' babies." Andrei: "And to your babies' babies' babies." And so on. It was kind of a joke. After all, everyone jokes about their work, even people in the extinction business. They said it, let off steam. To stay sane.

I am a schizophrenic and my thoughts would be mad anyway (I know this, using *insight*), but there are mad thoughts everywhere now and at least mine are mine, not manmade, like Francesca's, all ditties and jingles and lies. Uncle Ned has run away with the idea that I have a reality problem. Oh yeah? *Reality* has the reality problem. Reality is right out of control and could try anything, anytime. It is like the lake, always ready to explode. Ned will understand this all too well when I tell him—and I will tell him soon—that the baby has schizophrenia.

## Ned's Diary

*July 27.* Benson Holloway says he'll give me $150 for the jeep and I have half a mind to accept. If I strip off the plates and use it only on the property then I don't pay tax or insurance—but the old crate still guzzles money anyway. In this weather it overheats in five minutes and starts to drip and gurgle with gook and fumes. Just coming back from town you have to drive with your head practically out the window. But Benson is a shrewd bastard and why is *he* interested? This time next summer, though, I'll have to pay somebody to come and haul it away. Hell, I'll take the $150 and look around for something more practical. Mother and baby blooming (Fran sleepily, Harriet noisily!) and Dan absolutely no problem. The sun is really going it. You look up there and you think—the sun is really going it. The sun is really going nuclear.

## Dan's Notebook

Paradoxically, or at any rate surprisingly, the sun is powered by the weak force.

It is fueled by particle decay. If you want to witness nuclear fusion, then take a look at the sun. Ah, but you can't. Even at a distance of ninety million miles, it still hurts the eye. A thermonuclear detonation gives rise to temperatures appreciably greater than those to be found in the sun's core—or anywhere else in the universe, except for transient phenomena like exploding stars. At the Section one time, Dad showed me a film of a steel ball undergoing a significant fraction of this superstellar heat. It liquefies, and bubbles, like boiling water. And now the lake looks like boiling steel, what with the sun piling into it day after day.

Harriet, they tell me, was a premature baby. Well she has certainly made up for lost time. Many people believe that schizophrenia is a postadolescent occurrence. They are mistaken. An infant can show schizophrenic symptoms at a mere eight weeks. Harriet is eight months gone now and the condition is already far advanced. I'm afraid she is more or less a classic case.

*Deviant pattern of receptor preferences.* If you give her a rattle or a toy or anything else, what does she do? She shakes it, sniffs it, and puts it in her mouth. Thus the higher functions of vision and audition are rejected in favor of touch, taste, and smell.

*Repetitive and stereotyped behavioral patterns.* For meaninglessly long periods she bangs on flat surfaces with her palms. She shows a tragic failure to learn from her own errors. While babbling, she indulges in a random series of identical noises—then forgets them and starts making new ones!

*Faulty depth perception.* The baby shows early signs of deviant ambulation. She falls over all the time and bumps into things because, to her, spatial relationships are unstable and contingent.

*Motor-normalcy loss and abrupt personality mutation.* Often when Fran is trying to change her or clothe her or feed her or wipe her or indeed do anything which requires the baby's passive cooperation, Harriet will suddenly resist. She will go stiff, or flaccid, thus characteristically alternating between the rigid and the overrelaxed.

I could go on: time disperception, the way she often

interprets humor as insult, her interludes of excessive affection, the hypomania that prevents her from sleeping. Of course, the baby is perfectly well aware that I am onto her, and that is why she has turned against me at night. She has deceived her parents very cleverly—schizophrenics often show great cunning—and I don't think either Fran or Ned suspects for a moment that the baby can talk.

### Ned's Diary

*August 1.* A pinch and a punch, the first of the month. Born four weeks early on New Year's Day, the baby is now two-thirds of a year old. Keep it up, Hattie. . . . Fran tells me of a rather spooky conversation she had with Dan. It happened while she was feeding the baby in the living room. Apparently Dan starts in by saying that he thinks he's a homosexual! Just blurts it out. Strange, the new precocity —they all feel they're wised-up in their heads. Fran asked him his reasons for thinking this and Dan shrugged, admitting that he had never had a homosexual experience or encounter of any kind. He said it was to do with his "histamine count"—at least, that's how Fran remembers it. Also he accidentally busted her in the tub the other day. Fran says he was out of that door like a scalded cat. Now he leaves the room or turns his chair around whenever Fran hikes her shirt to give the baby a suck. He *does* say the damnedest things, and not all of them are off the wall by any means—he's bright, no question about it. This morning at breakfast I was fanning myself and scratching my hair over some new baby-battering atrocity in the newspaper and I said—Is it just me, or the media, or is there a boom in child abuse?

And Dan said, "It's exponential, like everything else these days." Himself a hostage to heredity, Dan naturally argued that if you abuse your children, well, then they will abuse theirs. It adds up. In fact it multiplies. Yes, but would that make any difference proportionately? Do people who abuse their children have more children than people who don't? I'm not sure how the math pans out on this, but maybe the kid is onto something. Sold the jeep. $125. Benson Hollo-way is a canny sonofabitch and you never know what he's planning or where he's really coming from. Still great, great heat. I don't think the sun can keep this up much longer.

### Dan's Notebook

In common with Harriet, or *Hattie,* the "baby," I have had no sleep for four nights.

But who needs it? True, I sometimes achieve unpleasant half-states that are further from wakefulness than from its opposite. Often, now, when I jerk upright in my bed, the baby is hiding nearby. I hope she will soon tire of this vicious frolic or tedious torture. My *insight,* though cer-tainly a remarkable tool, is no help to me here. Of course whenever I rouse myself, with infinite pain and difficulty, and get up and go to her room, the baby is back in her crib. She lies there and pretends to be asleep. I watch over her for hours but she never weakens in her imposture. Schizo-phrenics can do this because, you see, they don't *need* sleep. And when at last I return to bed she comes creeping in immediately. The baby is trying to make me do something that I will never do.

Thwarted in her plans and ambitions, Francesca is

wounded and remote, and feigns indifference. She concentrates on the baby in that finessing, wouldn't-you-know strategy always employed by females and fate. Ned is understandably angry about this too. He wanted Fran to take me as her lover; he is so old that he cannot expect to satisfy her for very much longer. So Uncle Ned ignores me, furiously busying himself elsewhere. All day I am very nice to the baby, repeatedly imploring her not to come to me at night. But she takes no notice and just pretends to be an unexceptional little creature called Harriet. When she does reveal her feelings, when she stares at me with a scowl of almost farcical hatred, they just think she's crying, like a baby.

They all seem to love each other here and maybe that's the point I'm missing. Ned loves Fran, who loves Harriet, who loves Fran, who loves Ned, who loves Harriet, who loves Ned. You know, through all this somber torment and disgusting confusion I sometimes imagine that if I weren't so sick I'd just be feeling lovelorn, love-beleaguered. I'd just be lovesick. Dad is gone, and my mother, so to speak, has always been conspicuous by her absence. I'd just be lovesick. For when it comes to the love match around here, I have lost, I am wiped out, love-six, love-six, love-six.

Even with my *time disperception* I know that I spend hours contemplating the firebreaks of the water. *Insight.* Will I cross them? Together the bugs and fauna in the wood make a noise like a great dry-hinged door slowly closing forever, closing ahead of me, closing behind me. Loathed am I too by the fierce and beautiful dragonflies that keep guard over Flame Lake.

*Ned's Diary*

*August 5.* Dan is kind of gruff or matter-of-fact with the
baby—but extraordinarily gentle. When Harriet, pleased
to see Dan, opens her arms to him from her highchair, his
face is studious as he bends to pick her up, and he shows the
extra care of the clumsy person, feeling in her armpits to get
the balance just right before hoisting her skyward, anxious
not to strain those little joints. Out on the scorched lakefront, when the baby is kneeling there and stuffing God
knows what into her mouth, or crawling at top speed toward
the water, Dan is always in frowning attendance and never
lets her out of his sight. I notice that he talks to her a lot,
and that's good, because I don't. Harriet adores him. It's
beautiful to see. Fran and I can think of no more natural
therapy, no simpler recommendation of life and living, than
to be with a baby as it makes its first acquaintance with the
world. . . . I don't know about this "exponential" business. Maybe there's just more of every kind of crap these
days. I've been badly disturbed by that case of the four-year-
old girl and her stepfather, step-uncle, and step-grand-
father. Every night they—No. Clearly, we cannot think
about that. But we can think about this: the great eyes of
the child when they open and focus, as the first of the men
enters the room. Thought the weather was breaking.
Wrong. We will obviously have to take this heat until the
end of time. Saw Benson Holloway sailing out of town in
the jeep. He must have been doing sixty-five. Dan's bites
are back.

### Dan's Notebook

Only the mosquitoes love me. Only the mosquitoes love my blood.

I look up from writing those words and on the other side of the wire screen eight or nine of them are clustered, two feet away, forming the shape of my face as surely as the stars delineate Draco, the firebreather, up in the circumpolar heavens. They are waiting. Soon I will go to them, my pretty ones. With the help of my *size inconstancy* they will change, in far less than a second, from flecks of foulness to horn-nosed hummingbirds as they settle and sip (heat-seeking, blood-seeking) on my open face.

The pile of the lake grows critical. And the baby is asking me why I am waiting.

"Tyramine," she will typically begin (after calling my name for hour after hour). "Bufotenine. Sorotonin. Malvaria. Reserpine. Spermadine. Tyramine."

Later I looked up and the "baby" was standing over my bed. With tears stinging the bites on my cheeks I begged her to return quietly to her room and cease this miserable experiment, but her eyes were lit by all the glitter-sizzle of schizophrenia as she told me how—together—we might end our trial by fire. She wants me to take her out into the sleeping warhead of Flame Lake, and so foreclose the great suspense. Even now, in the dead of night, as we both knew, the water would be black and boiling like vulcan pitch while, above, the leptons of the stars warily encircled the waiting Earth and its strong force. Toward dawn she left me, with a warning. But I know tonight I must decide.

I think it's cruel and senseless that in the daytime, when

we might discuss things rather more sensibly, the baby just lies there smiling and pretends to be a baby.

### Ned's Diary

*August 6.* I ought to describe this morning's events in as much detail as I can muster. I rose at eight and fixed a pot of coffee, Fran being something of a late starter, since the baby. Apparently Dan was not yet up, which surprised me —he is usually there in the kitchen, patiently waiting. I drank a cup and looked out into Flame Lake. And into broken weather. The water was heavily cured in mist, its colorlessness touched with dabs of silver, dabs of gold. I remember thinking: So the lake was a dud, a fizzle—it never quite went off. I opened the door to Dan's room and the coffee cup dropped from my hand and broke, silently, so it seemed. The bedclothes and curtains had been torn to pieces, torn to rags. As I stood there and stared I had the sense of great violence, violence compressed and controlled —everything was scrunched up, squeezed, strangled, impacted, imploded. Yes, and there were bites on the wooden surfaces, deep bites, and long scratch marks on the walls. I went outside and at once I saw his thin body, face-down in the shallows. . . . I woke Fran. I called Sheriff Groves. I called Dr. Slizard, who showed shock but no surprise. Then we straightened the whole thing out. Fortunately it would seem that the baby slept through it all. She's fine, and the commotion hasn't appeared to unsettle her. She just looks around every now and then, wonderingly—for him, for Dan. Sweet Jesus, the poor, poor kid. He would have been thirteen in January.

I don't know what is wrong. I have just read Dan's note-book, before sending it off to Slizard at the Section, as requested. I feel a fool, and an old one. To a culpable extent I lacked—I lacked insight. And what else? I have just read Dan's notebook and all I have in my head is a thought straight out of left field. Yesterday, at breakfast, Dan was there. As he drank his juice he gazed at the backs of the cereal boxes. What could be more—what could be more natural? I used to do that myself as a kid: toy-aircraft designs, send-in competitions, funnies, waffle and cookie recipes. But now? On the back of the high-fiber bran package there are dietary tips for avoiding cancer. On the back of the half-gallon carton of homogenized, pasteurized, vitamin D-fortified milk there are two mugshots of smiling children, gone, missing. (Have You Seen Them?). Date of birth, 7/7/79. Height, 3'6". Hair, brown. Eyes, blue. Missing, and missed, too, I'll bet—oh, most certainly. Done away with, probably, fucked and thrown over a wall somewhere, fucked and murdered, yeah, that's the most likely thing. I don't know what is wrong.

# THE TIME

---

# DISEASE

---

Twenty-twenty, and the *time* disease is epidemic. In my credit group, anyway. And yours too, friend, unless I miss my guess. Nobody thinks about anything else anymore. Nobody even pretends to think about anything else anymore. Oh yeah, except the sky, of course. The poor sky. . . . It's a thing. It's a situation. We all think about *time,* catching *time,* coming down with *time. I'm* still okay, I think, for the time being.

I took out my hand mirror. Everybody carries at least one hand mirror now. On the zip trains you see whole carloads jackknifed over in taut scrutiny of their hairlines and eye sockets. The anxiety is as electric as the twanging cable above our heads. They say more people are laid low by *time-*anxiety than by *time* itself. But only *time* is fatal. It's a problem, we agree, a definite feature. How can you change the subject when there's only one subject? People don't want to talk about the sky. They don't want to talk about the sky, and I don't blame them.

I took out my hand mirror and gave myself a ten-second scan: lower gumline, left eyelash count. I felt so heartened that I moved carefully into the kitchen and cracked out a beer. I ate a *hero,* and a *ham salad.* I lit another cigarette. I activated the TV and keyed myself in to the Therapy Channel. I watched a seventy-year-old documentary about a road-widening scheme in a place called Orpington, over in England there. . . . Boredom is meant to be highly prophylactic when it comes to *time.* We are all advised to experience as much boredom as we possibly can. To bore somebody is said to be even more sanative than to be bored oneself. That's why we're always raising our voices in company and going on and on about anything that enters our heads. Me I go on about *time* the whole time: a reckless habit. Listen to me. I'm at it again.

The outercom sounded. I switched from Therapy to Intake. No visual. "Who is it?" I asked the TV. The TV told me. I sighed and put the call on a half-minute hold. Soothing music. Boring music. . . . Okay—you want to hear my theory? Now, some say that *time* was caused by congestion, air plague, city life (and city life is the only kind of life there is these days). Others say that *time* was a result of the first nuclear conflicts (limited theater, Persia *v.* Pakistan, Zaire *v.* Nigeria, and so on, no really big deal or anything: they took the heat and the light, and we took the cold and the dark; it helped fuck the sky, that factor) and more particularly of the saturation TV coverage that followed: all day the screen writhed with flesh, flesh dying or living in a queer state of age. Still others say that *time* was an evolutionary consequence of humankind's ventures into space (they shouldn't have gone out there, what with things so rocky back home). *Food,* pornography, the cancer cure. . . . Me I think it was the twentieth century that did it. The twentieth century was all it took.

"Hi there, Happy," I said. "What's new?"

". . . Lou?" her voice said warily. "Lou, I don't feel so good."

"That's not new. That's old."

"I don't feel so good. I think it's really happening this time."

"Oh, sure."

Now this was Happy Farraday. That's right: the TV star. *The* Happy Farraday. Oh, we go way back, Happy and me.

"Let's take a look at you," I said. "Come on, Happy, give me a visual on this."

The screen remained blank, its dead cells seeming to squirm or hover. On impulse I switched from Intake to Daydrama. There was Happy, full face to camera, vividly doing her thing. I switched back. Still no visual. I said, "I just checked you out on the other channel. You're in superb shape. What's your factor?"

"It's here," said her voice. "It's *time.*"

TV stars are especially prone to *time*-anxiety—to *time* too, it has to be said. Why? Well, I think we're looking at an occupational hazard here. It's a thing. True, the work could hardly be more boring. Not many people know this, but all the characters in the Armchair, Daydrama, and Proscenium channels now write their own lines. It's a new gimmick, intended to promote formlessness, to combat sequentiality, and so on: the target-research gurus have established that this goes down a lot better with the homebound. Besides, all the writing talent is in game-conception or mass-therapy, doing soothe stuff for the nonemployed and other sections of the populace that are winding down from being functional. There are fortunes to be made in the leisure and assuagement industries. The standout writers are like those teenage billionaires in the early days of the chip revolution. On the other hand, making money—like reading and writing, come to that—dangerously increases your *time*-anxiety levels. Obviously. The more money you have, the more time you have to worry about *time*. It's a thing. Happy Farraday is top credit, and she also bears the weight of TV fame (where millions know you or think they do), that collective sympathy, identification, and concern that, I suspect, seriously depletes your *time*-resistance. I've started to keep a kind of file on this. I'm beginning to think of it as reciprocity syndrome, one of the new—

Where was I? Yeah. On the line with Happy here. My mind has a tendency to wander. Indulge me. It helps, *time*-wise.

"Okay. You want to tell me what symptoms you got?" She told me. "Call a doctor," I joked. "Look, give me a break. This is—what? The second time this year? The third?"

"It's different this time."

"It's the new role, Happy. That's all it is." In her new

series on Daydrama, Happy was playing the stock part of a glamorous forty-year-old with a bad case of *time*-anxiety. And it was getting to her—of course it was. "You know where I place the blame? On your talent! As an actress you're just too damn good. Greg Buzhardt and I were—"

"Save it, Lou," she said. "Don't bore me out. It's real. It's *time*."

"I know what you're going to do. I know what you're going to do. You're going to ask me to drive over."

"I'll pay."

"It's not the money, Happy, it's the time."

"Take the dollar lane."

"Wow," I said. "You're, you must be kind of serious this time."

So I stood on the shoulder, waiting for Roy to bring up my Horsefly from the stacks. Well, Happy is an old friend and one of my biggest clients, also an ex-wife of mine, and I had to do the right thing. For a while out there I wasn't sure what time it was supposed to be or whether I had a day or night situation on my hands—but then I saw the faint tremors and pulsings of the sun, up in the east. The heavy green light sieved down through the ripped and tattered troposphere, its fissures as many-eyed as silk or pantyhose, with a liquid quality too, churning, changing. Green light: let's go. . . . I had a bad scare myself the other week, a very bad scare. I was in bed with Danuta and we were going to have a crack at making love. Okay, a dumb move—but it was her birthday, and we'd been doing a lot of tranquilizers

that night. I don't happen to believe that lovemaking is
quite as risky as some people say. To hear some people talk,
you'd think that sex was a suicide pact. To hold hands is to
put your life on the line. "Look at the *time*-fatality figures
among the under classes," I tell them. They screw like
there's no tomorrow, and do they come down with *time?*
No, it's us high-credit characters who are really at risk. Like
me and Danuta. Like Happy. Like you. . . . Anyway, we
were lying on the bed together, as I say, seminude, and
talking about the possibility of maybe getting into the right
frame of mind for a little of the old pre-foreplay—when all
of a sudden I felt a rosy glow break out on me like sweat.
There was this clogged inner heat, a heavy heat, with something limitless in it, right in the crux of my being. Well, I
panicked. You always tell yourself you're going to be brave,
dignified, stoical. I ran wailing into the bathroom. I yanked
open the triple mirror; the automatic scanlight came on
with a crackle. I opened my eyes and stared. There I stood,
waiting. Yes, I was clear, I was safe. I broke down and wept
with relief. After a while Danuta helped me back into bed.
We didn't try to make love or anything. No *way*. I felt too
damn good. I lay there dabbing my eyes, so happy, so
grateful—my old self again.

"You screw much, Roy?"

"—Sir?"

"You screw much, Roy?"

"Some. I guess."

Roy was an earnest young earner of the stooped, musta-
chioed variety. He seemed to have burdensome responsibil-
ities; he even wore his cartridge belt like some kind of hernia

strap or spinal support. This was the B-credit look, the buffer-class look. Pretty soon, they project, society will be equally divided into three sections. Section B will devote itself entirely to defending section A from section C. I'm section A. I'm glad I have Roy and his boys on my side.

"Where you driving to today, sir?" he asked as he handed me my car card.

"Over the hills and far away, Roy. I'm going to see Happy Farraday. Any message?"

Roy looked troubled. "Sir," he said, "you got to tell her about Duncan. The new guy at the condo. He has an alcohol thing. Happy Farraday doesn't know about it yet. Duncan, he sets fire to stuff, with his problem there."

"His problem, Roy? That's harsh, Roy."

"Well, okay. I don't want to do any kind of value thing here. Maybe it was, like when he was a kid or something. But Duncan has an alcohol situation there. That's the truth of it, Mr. Goldfader. And Happy Farraday doesn't know about it yet. You got to warn her. You got to warn her, sir —right now, before it's too late."

I gazed into Roy's handsome, imploring, deeply stupid face. The hot eyes, the tremulous cheeks, the mustache. Jesus Christ, what difference do these guys think a *mustache* is going to make to anything? For the hundredth time I said to him, "Roy, it's all made up. It's just TV, Roy. She writes that stuff herself. It isn't real."

"Now I don't know about none of that," he said, his hand splayed in quiet propitiation. "But I'd feel better in my mind if you'd warn her about Duncan's factor there."

Roy paused. With some difficulty he bent to dab at an

oil stain on his superwashable blue pants. He straightened
up with a long wheeze. Being young, Roy was, of course,
incredibly fat—for reasons of *time*. We both stood there and
gazed at the sky, at the spillages, the running colors, at the
great chemical betrayals. . . .

"It's bad today," said Roy. "Sir? Mr. Goldfader? Is it true
what they say, that Happy Farraday's coming down with
*time?*"


Traffic was light and I was over at Happy's before I knew it.
Traffic *is* a problem, as everybody keeps on saying. It's okay,
though, if you use the more expensive lanes. We have a five-
lane system here in our county: free, nickel, dime, quarter,
and dollar (that's nothing, five, ten, twenty-five, or a
hundred dollars a mile)—but of course the free lane is non-
operational right now, a gridlock, a caravan, a linear break-
ers' yard of slumped and frazzled heaps, dead rolling stock
that never rolls. They're going to have a situation there with
the nickel lane too, pretty soon. The thing about driving
anywhere is, it's so unbelievably boring. Here's another
plus: since the ban on rearview mirrors, there's not much
scope for any *time*-anxiety. They had to take the mirrors
away, yes sir. They got my support on that. The concentra-
tion-loss was a real feature, you know, driving along and
checking out your crow's feet and hair-line, all at the same
time. There used to be a party atmosphere out on the
throughway, in the cheap lanes where mobility is low or
minimal. People would get out of their cars and horse
around. Maybe it still goes on, for all I know. The dividing

barriers are higher now, with the new Boredom Drive, and
you can't really tell what gives. I *did* see something interesting though. I couldn't help it. During the long wait at the
security intersect, where even the dollar lane gets loused up
by all the towtrucks and ambulances—and by the great
fleets of copbikes and squadcars—I saw three *runners,* three
*time* punks, loping steadily across the disused freightlane,
up on the East Viaduct. There they were, as plain as day:
shorts, sweatshirts, *running*-shoes. The stacked cars all
sounded their horns, a low furious bellow from the old
beasts in their stalls. A few dozen cops appeared with bull-
horns and tried to talk them down—but they just gestured
and *ran* defiantly on. They're sick in the head, these punks,
though I guess there's a kind of logic in it somewhere. They
do vitamins, you know. Yeah. They work out and screw
around; they have their nihilistic marathons. I saw one up
close down at the studios last week. A security guard found
her *running* along the old outer track. They asked her some
questions and then let her go. She was about thirty, I guess.
She looked in terrible shape.

And so I drove on, without incident. But even through
the treated glass of the windshield I could see and sense the
atrocious lancings and poppings in the ruined sky. It gets
to you. Stare at the blazing noon of a high-watt bulb for ten
or fifteen minutes then shut your eyes, real tight and sudden. That's what the sky looks like. You know, we pity it,
or at least I do. I look at the sky and I just think . . . *ow.*
Whew. Oh, the sky, the poor *sky.*

Happy Farraday had left a priority clearance for me at Realty HQ, so I didn't have to hang around that long. To tell you the truth, I was scandalized by how lax and perfunctory the security people were becoming. It's always like this, after a quiet few weeks. Then there's another shitstorm from Section C, and all the writs start flying around again. In the cubicle I put my clothes back on and dried my hair. While they okayed my urinalysis and x-ray congruence tests, I watched TV in the commissary. I sat down, delicately, gingerly (you know how it is, after a strip search), and took three clippings out of my wallet. These are for the file. What do you think?

Item 1, from the news page of *Screen Week:*

In a series of repeated experiments at the Valley Chemistry Workshop, Science Student Edwin Navasky has "proven" that hot water freezes faster than cold. Said Edwin, "We did the test four times." Added Student Adviser Joy Broadener: "It's a feature. We're real baffled."

Item 2, from the facts section of *Armchair Guide:*

Candidate Day McGwire took out a spot on Channel 29 last Monday. Her purpose: to deny persistent but unfounded rumors that she suffered from heart trouble. Sadly, she was unable to appear. The reason: her sudden hospitalization with a cardiac problem.

Item 3, from the update column of *Television:*

Meteorological Pilot Lars Christer reported another sighting of "The Thing Up There" during a routine low-level flight. The location: 10,000 feet above Lake Baltimore. His description: "It was kind of oval, with kind of a black circle in the center." The phenomenon is believed to be a cumulus or spore formation. Christer's reaction: "I don't know what to make of it. It's a thing."

"Goldfader," roared the tannoy, scattering my thoughts. The caddycart was ready at the gate. In the west now the heavens looked especially hellish and distraught, with a throbbing, peeled-eyeball effect on the low horizon— bloodshot, conjunctivitic. Pink eye. The Thing Up There, I sometimes suspect, it might look like an eye, flecked with painful tears, staring, incensed. . . . Using my cane I walked cautiously around the back of Happy's bungalow. Her twenty-year-old daughter Sunny was lying naked on a lounger, soaking up the haze. She made no move to cover herself as I limped poolside. Little Sunny here wants me to represent her someday, and I guess she was showing me the goods. Well it's like they say: if you've got it, flaunt it.

"Hi, Lou," she said sleepily. "Take a drink. Go ahead. It's five o'clock."

I looked at Sunny critically as I edged past her to the bar. The kid was a real centerfold, no question. Now don't misunderstand me here. I say *centerfold,* but of course pornography hasn't really kept pace with *time.* At first they tried filling the magazines and mature cable channels with newlook women, like Sunny, but it didn't work out. *Time* has effectively killed pornography, except as an underground blood sport, or a punk thing. *Time* has killed much else. Here's an interesting topic sentence. Now that masturbation is the only form of sex that doesn't carry a government health warning, what do we think about when we're doing it there, what is *left* for us to think about? Me, I'm not saying. Christ, are *you?* What images slide, what specters flit . . . what happens to these thoughts as they hover and mass, up there in the blasted, the totaled, up there in the fucked sky?

"Come on, Sunny. Where's your robe."

As I fixed myself a vodka-context and sucked warily on a *pretzel,* I noticed Sunny's bald patch gently gleaming in the mist. I sighed.

"You like my dome?" she asked, without turning. "Relax, it's artificial." She sat up straight now and looked at me coyly. She smiled. Yeah, she'd had her teeth gimmicked too—by some cowboy snaggle-artist down in the Valley, no doubt. I poled myself poolside again and took a good slow scan. The flab and pallor were real all right, but the stretch marks seemed cosmetic: too symmetrical, too pronounced.

"Now, you listen to me, kid," I began. "Here are the realities. To scudbathe, to flop out all day by the pool with a bottle or two, to take on a little weight around the middle there—that's good for a girl. I mean you got to keep in shape. But this mutton routine, Sunny, it's for the punks. No oldjob ever got on my books and no oldjob ever will. Here are the reasons. Number one—" And I gave young Sunny a long talking-to out there, a real piece of my mind. I had her in the boredom corner and I wasn't letting her out. I went on and on at her—on and on and on and on. Me, I almost checked out myself, as boredom edged toward despair (the way boredom will), gazing into the voided pool, the reflected skyscape, and the busy static, in the sediment of sable rain.

"Yeah, well," I said, winding up. "Anyway. What's the thing? You look great."

She laughed, coughed, and spat. "Forget it, Lou," she said croakily. "I only do it for fun."

"I'm glad to hear that, Sunny. Now where's your mother."

"Two days."

"Uh?"

"In her room. In her room two days. She's serious this time."

"Oh, sure."


I rebrimmed my drink and went inside. The only point of light in the hallway came from the mirror's sleepless scan-lamp. I looked myself over as I limped by. The heavy bore-dom and light stress of the seven-hour drive had done me good. I was fine, fine. "Happy?" I said, and knocked.

"Is that you, Lou?" The voice was strong and clear—and it was quick, too. Direct, alert. "I'll unlatch the door, but don't come in right away."

"Sure," I said. I took a pull of booze and groped around for a chair. But then I heard the click and Happy's brisk "Okay" . . . Now I have to tell you that two things puzzled me here. First, the voice; second, the alacrity. Usually when she's in this state you can hardly hear the woman, and it takes an hour or more for her to get to the door and back into bed again. Yeah, I thought, she must have been waiting with her fingers poised on the handle. There's nothing wrong with Happy. The lady is fine, fine.

So in I went. She had the long black nets up over the sack —streaming, glistening, a crib for the devil's progeny. I moved through the gloom to the bedside chair and sat myself down with a grunt. A familiar chair. A familiar vigil.

"Mind if I don't smoke?" I asked her. "It's not the lungburn. I just get tuckered out lighting the damn things all the time. Understand what I mean?"

No answer.

"How are you feeling, Happy?"

No answer.

"Now listen, kid. You got to quit this nonsense. I know it's problematic with the new role and everything, but— do I have to tell you again what happened to Day Montague? Do I, Happy? Do I? You're forty years old. You look fantastic. Let me tell you what Greg Buzhardt said to me when he saw the outtakes last week. He said, 'Style. Class. Presence. Sincerity. Look at the ratings. Look at the profiles. Happy Farraday is the woman of men's dreams.' That's what he said. 'Happy Farraday is the—' "

"*Lou.*"

The voice came from behind me. I swiveled and felt the twinge of tendons in my neck. Happy stood in a channel of bathroom light and also in the softer channel or haze of her slip of silk. She stood there as vivid as health itself, as graphic as youth, with her own light sources, the eyes, the mouth, the hair, the dips and curves of the flaring throat. The silk fell to her feet, and the glass fell from my hand, and something else dropped or plunged inside my chest.

"Oh, Christ," I said. "Happy, I'm sorry."

---

I remember what the sky was like, when the sky was young
—its shawls and fleeces, its bears and whales, its cusps and
clefts. A sky of gray, a sky of blue, a sky of spice. But now
the sky has gone, and we face different heavens. Some vital
casing has left our lives. Up there now, I think, a kind of
turnaround occurs. *Time*-fear collects up there and comes
back to us in the form of *time*. It's the sky, the sky, it's the
fucking *sky*. If enough people believe that a thing is real or
happening, then it seems that the thing must happen, must
go for real. Against all odds and expectation, these are
magical times we're living in: proletarian magic. Gray
magic!

Now that it's over, now that I'm home and on the mend,
with Danuta back for good and Happy gone forever, I think
I can talk it all out and tell you the real story. I'm sitting on
the cramped veranda with a blanket on my lap. Before me
through the restraining bars the sunset sprawls in its polluted pomp, full of genies, cloaked ghosts, crimson demons
of the middle sky. Red light: let's stop—let's end it. The
Thing Up There, it may not be God, of course. It may
be the Devil. Pretty soon, Danuta will call me in for my
*broth*. Then a nap, and an hour of TV maybe. The Therapy
Channel. I'm really into early nights. . . . This afternoon
I went walking, out on the shoulder. I don't know why.
I don't think I'll do it again. On my return Roy appeared and helped me into the lift. He then asked me
shyly,

"Happy Farraday—she okay now, sir?"

"Okay?" I said. "Okay? What do you mean, *okay?* You never read a news page, Roy?"

"When she had to leave for Australia there. I wondered if she's okay. It'll be better for her, I guess. She was in a situation, with Duncan. It was a thing there."

"That's just TV, for Christ's sake. They wrote her out," I said, and felt a sudden, leaden calm. "She's not in Australia, Roy. She's in heaven."

"—Sir?"

"She's *dead,* God damn it."

"Now I don't know about none of that," he said, with one fat palm raised. "All it is is, I just hope she's okay, over in Australia there."

Happy is in heaven, or I hope she is. I hope she's not in hell. Hell is the evening sky and I surely hope she's not up there. Ah, how to bear it? It's a thing. No, it really is.

I admit right now that I panicked back there, in the bungalow bedroom with the chute of light, the altered woman, and my own being so quickly stretched by fragility and fear. I shouted a lot. *Lie down! Call Trattman! Put on your robe!* That kind of thing. "Come on, Lou. Be realistic," she said. "Look at me." And I looked. Yeah. Her skin had that shiny telltale succulence, all over. Her hair—which a week ago, God damn it, lay as thin and colorless as my own —was humming with body and glow. And the mouth, Christ, lips all full and wet, and an animal tongue, like a heart, not Happy's, the tongue of another woman, bigger, greedier, younger. Younger. Classic *time.* Oh, classic.

She had me go over and lie down on the bed with her

there, to give comfort, to give some sense of final safety. I was in a ticklish state of nerves, as you'd imagine. *Time* isn't infectious (we do know *that* about *time*) but sickness in any form won't draw a body nearer and I wanted all my distance. *Stay out,* it says. Then I saw—I saw it in her breasts, high but heavy, their little points tender, detailed, *time*-inflamed; and the smell, the smell of deep memory, tidal, submarine . . . I knew the kind of comfort she wanted. Yes, and *time* often takes them this way, I thought, in my slow and stately terror. You've come this far: go further, I told myself. Go closer, nearer, closer. Do it for her, for her and for old times' sake. I stirred, ready to let her have all that head and hand could give, until I too felt the fever in my lines of heat, the swell and smell of youth and death. This is suicide, I thought, and I don't care. . . . At one point, during the last hours, just before dawn, I got to my feet and crept to the window and looked up at the aching, the hurting sky; I felt myself gray and softly twanging for a moment, like a coathanger left to shimmer on the pole, with Happy there behind me, alone in her bed and her hot death. "Honey," I said out loud, and went to join her. I like it, I thought, and gave a sudden nod. What do I like? I like the love. This is suicide and I don't care.

I was in terrible shape, mind you, for the next couple of months, really beat to shit, out of it, just out of it. I would wake at seven and leap out of the sack. I suffered energy attacks. Right off my *food,* I craved thick meat and thick wine. I couldn't watch any Therapy. After barely a half-hour of some home-carpentry show or marathon dance contest I'd be pacing the room with frenzy in my bitten fingertips. I put Danuta at risk too, on several occasions. I even threw a pass in on little Sunny Farraday, who moved in here for a time after the cremation. Danuta divorced me. She even moved out. But she's back now. She's a good kid, Danuta—she helped me through. The whole thing is behind me now, and I think (knock on wood) that I'm more or less my old self again.

Pretty soon I'll rap on the window with my cane and have Danuta fetch me another blanket. Later, she'll help me inside for my *broth*. Then a nap, and an hour of TV maybe. The Therapy Channel. I'm happy here for the time being, and willingly face the vivid torment, the boiling acne of the dying sky. When this sky is dead, will they give us a new one? Today my answering service left a strange message: I have to call a number in Sydney, over in Australia there. I'll do it tomorrow. Or the next day. Yeah. I can't make the effort right now. To reach for my stick, to lift it, to rap the glass, to say *Danuta*—even that takes steep ascents of time. All things happen so slowly now. I have a new feature with my back. I broke a tooth last week on a piece of *toast*. Jesus, how I hate bending and stairs. The sky hangs above me in shredded webs, in bloody tatters. It's a big relief, and I'm grateful. I'm okay. I'm good, good. For the time being, at any rate, I show no signs of coming down with *time*.

# THE LITTLE
## PUPPY
## THAT COULD

The little puppy came bounding and tumbling over the fallow fields. Here he comes, bounding, tumbling. Like all the most adorable little puppies, this little puppy had large pleading brown eyes, wobbly half-cocked ears, and loose folds of flesh on the join of his neck. His coat was a subtle gray (like silver in shadow), with a triangle of white on his chest, like a shirtfront, and white tufts on each paw, like socks, like shoes, like little spats! He was a bit plump, this little puppy, it had to be said—but adorably so. Puppy fat, not doggy fat. He had been running and running for days and days. Where had the little puppy come from? Where was the little puppy heading, and so eagerly? His proud tail high, his front paws gaily outthrust, his—whoops! Over he goes again. Then he's up, undismayed, bounding, tumbling, toward huge discoveries, toward wonderful transformations. Of course, the little puppy had no idea where he had come from or where he was heading. But he was going to get there.

Now, the puppy probably sniffed or sensed the village before he saw it—the fires, the crescents, the human place. In truth, his eyesight was not all that reliable, floppy, tousled, subject to passionate distortions of fear and desire. But he saw something new out there, shape and pattern, evidence, a great manifestation pressed or carved upon the random world through which he bounded. The little puppy tumbled to a halt, then wriggled himself upright. He knew at once that he had found the place that his heart sought— his destination. Down in the round valley he could descry moving figures, and circles within circles, and, at their crux, a flaming parabola shaped like a scythe: a swan neck, a query of fire! The little puppy stood there, anxiously snapping his jaws. His head craned forward, urging the little puppy on, but his paws just jostled and danced. His tail started wagging, hesitantly at first, then with such reckless vigor that he almost pulled a muscle in his plump little rump. On he bounded, nearer, nearer, down through the dawn shadows, almost flying, his young blood aflame— until he saw a human group moving stolidly from a gateway in the low palisade. Now the little puppy really turned on the speed. He hurtled toward them, then leapt into the air and swiveled, skidlanding back-first at their feet—the four paws limply raised, the shivering tail, his soft belly exposed in reflexive surrender and trust.

And nothing happened. . . . The puppy awoke in a pool

of bafflement and hurt. He hadn't been asleep or anything, but life was like that for the little puppy, it all being so much more fervent down there, so pressing, so sudden. The people just stood there in a stoical arc, six or seven of them; some faces wore fear, some disgust; none showed kindness. At last the puppy climbed sadly to his feet and looked up at them with beseeching eyes, his worked jaw forming a question. His question was your question. Why should they want to act this way toward a little puppy, his puzzled heart full of bruised love, a puppy made for cuddles and romps? And the people had no answer. They too (the puppy seemed to sense) were full of confusion, full of pain. Wishing to comfort them, and hoping there had simply been some sort of misunderstanding, the little puppy crept forward again, in trembling supplication. But now the people began to turn away. The men mumbled and sneered. One woman wept; another woman spat—spat at the little puppy. Blinking, he watched them go through the gate. It was strange. The little puppy didn't know much but he did know this: that the people were not unkind. No, they were not. They were not unkind.

And so, keeping his distance, foraging for food (grubs, roots, a special kind of flower, certain intoxicating though regrettable substances that his nose liked but his tongue loathed), and with many an exhausted sigh, the little puppy padded around the human place, until the day began to turn. As he searched for the tongue-tickling ants and the fairy toast of butterflies among the rocks and hollows, he kept glancing hopefully toward the ringed settlement— itself a termitary, full of erratic yet significant motion. His hunger appeased, propitiated, the puppy waited, there on the hillside, watching, sighing. Despite his wretchedness he nursed an intense presentiment of great things, of marvelous revelations—a feeling that may well have been delusive, since he always had it. Later in the day he encountered a damp and steaming hillock whose very interesting smells he investigated busily. Moments later he found himself lying on his side, being helplessly sick. The little puppy kept away from that hillock and all others with the same smell, a smell he came to think of as meaning danger. As night fell in folds over the disquieted landscape, he heard from across the valley the frazzled snarling of a beast, tireless and incarnadine, a sound that chimed in his head with the jeopardy of the special smell. All the little puppy could see or hear of the village now was the dreadful fire, the long flaming curve at the heart of the human place.

It was love, unquestionably love, and with classic symptoms. Each morning the little girl came with her basket, over the hills and far away, to gather flowers, and to swim in the varnished creek. Her wandering gait brought her there, punctually (the day was always *exactly* the same color when she came), barefoot, in her white dress. The flowers themselves all swooned and pouted at her approach. They wanted to be picked. Pick *me*. The flowers, the fantastic flowers—watch them as they hobnob and canoodle in the haze! Imagine too the little puppy, staring out from the shadows of the secretive tree, his nose on his paws, his tail lazily swishing, the brown eyes all gooey and gummed.

Now he raised his head (the neck suddenly erect and astonished) as the young girl slipped out of her dress, tiptoed
naked into the shallow pool—and sang as she bathed her
breasts! The little puppy sighed. He loved her from his
distance, a love instant and wordless and full of hunger. He
would exchange the pigments and pain of life—and all its
great presentiments—for a single caress of her hand, a pat,
a smack. It was a love he would never show. People didn't
like him: he knew that by now. In the fields above the valley
he had approached at least a couple of dozen of them, singly
and in groups, assuming various styles and postures (crawling, strolling, skipping); in every case he had been thoroughly jeered and gestured-at for his pains—and they *were*
pains, and there were many of them now. So while every
cell in the little puppy's body desperately urged him to join
the young girl and her flowers, to declare himself, to gambol
and prance and snuggle and spoon, he stayed in his shadows
and loved from his distance. It was love, at any rate. And of
this the little puppy was sure: he would never settle for
anything less than love.

Transfigured, she climbed from the caressing water and
knelt on the bank to warm her body in the sun. Edging
forward an inch or two, a foot, a yard, the puppy kept his
vigil, sighing, wincing, smacking his jaws in sleepy fever.
For he was by now a rather sick little puppy—bruised and
pining, quite starved of the detailed tenderness that every
little puppy needs. And this morning he lay there doubly
traumatized by fear and relief. Violent events had forced
him actually to skip the assignation of the previous day;
and, in the little puppy's drowsy world of cause and effect,

he believed that if he failed to appear at the nervous creek then, well, the loved one would fail to appear also, would never reappear, would disappear forever. Hence his shock of relief, his seizure of consolation, when he peered out from the secretive shadows and saw her there once more.

It happened the night before the night before. It happened like this. The little puppy was soundly sleeping in his usual place (a sheltered hollow by a leaning tree) and in his usual posture (one of utter abandonment), when a flurry of sounds and smells suddenly wrestled him to his feet. Frowning, the little puppy registered curious stirrings in the texture of the earth, and sensed faint splittings and crashings, drawing nearer. The scent, still diluted by distance, keenly intrigued the puppy but also awakened in him the glands of danger. He hesitated, there in the changeable night. Too weak and confused to make a run for it, he eyed the burrow where he had recently spent a pleasant hour, sniffing and scratching and trying out a powerful new bark. Then the sounds were upon him: louder, worse, hot and toxic with limitless hunger. And still the little puppy hesitated, the head bending slightly in its trance, the tail twitching in a reflex of hope—of play. But now the gust of gas and blood swept over his coat: the little puppy slithered whimpering to the burrow and shouldered himself into the clinging damp. Or he tried. The locked front paws searched for purchase, yet that plump little rump of his was still exposed while the back legs skidded and thrashed. And now he could actually feel the torch of breath, the scalding saliva playing on his rear. Terror couldn't do it—but horror could. Horror gouged him into the earth with an audible

pop; and he lay there coughing and weeping until the egregious rage had vented, had wrecked itself on the ground
above his head. . . . So shaken was the little puppy that he
failed to emerge for a good thirty-six hours, and then only a
famished despair had him backing toward the daylight. It
wasn't easy getting into the burrow, but it was easy getting
out. For the little puppy, it seemed, was getting littler all
the time.

And so he sighed and gazed, and gazed and sighed. The
flowers had all lost their swoon and now arched and strained
to meet the young girl's touch. Oh, how they longed to be
picked. Light and naked she moved among them, leaning
to free a stem from the earth, then straightening to fix the
petals in her costly black hair. Loved by the little puppy
(mutely, proudly—how many lifetimes would he not joy-
ously spend, unrequited, unregarded, in this half-love, this
half-life?), the young girl sang, the young girl swam, the
young girl lay back on her dress, drying herself and dreaming of growth, of change, of mysterious metamorphoses.
Humming, murmuring, she sought another sun-dazed
shape in which to drowse, opened her eyes—and what
should she see? Why, a little puppy, a very tentative little
puppy, inching through the flowers, its tail anxiously shriv-
eled, the hot nose brushing the grass. The puppy had had
absolutely no intention of approaching the girl in this way.
But then, the puppy just found that he'd gone ahead and
done it—as little puppies will. The girl sat up and, with
no waste of attention, stared at him strictly, a hand raised
to her mouth. The little puppy, sensing the gravity of his
error, was about to slink miserably away, to the ends of the
earth, never to return—but then she laughed and said,

"Hello. Who are you then? Come on. Come here. It's all right. Ooh, what a funny little creature you are. . . . I'd take you home with me. But they won't like you. Because of the dog. Keithette won't like you. I don't think Tom will either. My name is Andromeda. And *I* like you. Yes, I really do."

All this of course was pure Greek to the little puppy— but who cared? Her voice, with its infant lilt and music, was just another vast extra in his ambient bower of bliss. Not in his dreams, in his wagging, whimpering dreams. . . . While it might be pushing it to say that little puppies have fantasies, it is certainly the case that they have sentiments, powerful ones too—down there, where everything rips and tears like hunger. Lying on his back among the envious flowers, her hand on his tummy (lightly steadied by a speculative paw), the tail in tune with the slow heartbeat, the little puppy fairly choked and drowned in his little sea of joy. Ah, the piercing peace. All covered in heaven— puppy heaven! For many hours they rolled and cuddled and snuggled and nuzzled, until the color of the day began to change.

"Oh no," said the girl.

She ran away in vivid terror. Told to stay, the little puppy followed her, as unobtrusively as possible, averting his glance whenever she turned to shoo him back (as though he believed that if he couldn't see her, then she couldn't see him). But now Andromeda paused in her flight and stood her ground to warn him.

"Stay. Be careful of the dog. Come tomorrow. Promise. Stay, but please don't go away. Stay! Oh *stay*."

Deeply puzzled, his tail uncertainly working, the little

puppy watched her run, down the valley toward the gaping
crater, where the fires were already boiling, black-veined,
as they started to consume the air of the dusk.


During the next wave or packet of time, the life of the little
puppy that could resembled a gorgeous and dreadful dream,
the two states—panic and rapture—welded as close as the
two faces of a knife; sometimes he felt his heart might crack
and ooze with the incredible uncertainty of it all. But, being
a puppy, he spent much of his time in the unaltered conditions, the extremes. When Andromeda loomed above him,
her sun-warmed hair patterned with magical flowers, when
she tickled both sets of ribs and kissed his hot belly, do you
think the little puppy was anything but definitively flat-
tened with joy? Life was all foreplay, wonderful foreplay.
The little puppy devised other games too: the game where
he ran very fast toward her and then veered off at the last
second; the game where he ran around her in concentric
circles wherever she went; the game where he ran away quite
languidly and then skipped out of reach when she approached; and so on. Andromeda seemed uncharacteristi-
cally slow to catch on to his games—perhaps because the
little puppy was so weak and sickly now, and so easily tired.
Yet he wouldn't stop. There was an edge of delirium in his
romps. Often, too, he came a cropper on some of his more
ambitious maneuvers. One afternoon, after hours of
prompting, she was persuaded to play the stick game,
whereby she threw a stick and the little puppy ran after it
—returning it to her, or not, depending on his puppyish

whim. By accident she once threw the stick into the creek, and the little puppy hurled himself in there after it. He appeared to be in some difficulties for a while; certainly he had quite a coughing fit on the bank when Andromeda hauled him out. She noticed then, as he lay recovering by her side, that his tail and back paws were badly scalded and enflamed. She looked down at him with a worried frown. The little puppy blinked up at her gratefully. Through the spokes of his wet lashes, and what with all the photospheric brilliance above and behind her, well, she looked—she looked to him like a stern and formidable angel, divine essence, a Power, a Dominion, a Throne, covered in prismatic jewelry, sliding down the sun's rays. Of course we must remember the little puppy's poor eyesight . . . oh, that *poor* little puppy.

Because the nights were so different, so much longer than the days (at least three times as long), and so full of fear. Squirming in his burrow, while the great animal, senior and atrocious, tore greedily at the narrow opening, the little puppy had no thoughts for the day—the distant, the derisory day. He didn't understand. How had he unleashed such rage in a creature which, or so he felt, he might have looked to for love, for protection, for play? He didn't understand. But he understood one thing; he made a certain distinction, a nice one too. The little puppy understood the difference between terror and horror. Terror was when the girl had gone and night began to come, wiping color from the world. Horror was when the beast was actually *there,* the flames of its breath at the opening of the burrow, the saliva that seared the little puppy's rump.

"This can't go on," said Andromeda one morning, when she found the little puppy sneezing and dozing and trembling by the nervous creek. He couldn't eat the food she had smuggled out for him. Reflexively he lifted himself up for a romp, but his hind legs gave way, and he rolled back on to the grass with a fatalistic sigh. Usually when she looked at the little puppy Andromeda always thought: life! Here is *life*. But now the possibility occurred to her (long-postponed, an idea that made her whole body bend with nausea) that the little puppy was dying. It could be that the little puppy just wasn't going to make it. For you understand that fear had quite emptied him—fear, and intense puppy loneliness, the need for inclusion, the need to be . . . inside.

Andromeda gulped and said, "I don't care. I'm taking you home with me. Now. I don't care."

And so, very, very carefully, Andromeda bedded down the little floppy-limbed puppy at the bottom of her basket, and covered his weak protesting form with flowers and white grapes and a pink handkerchief. The little puppy was slow to understand this game and would persistently writhe and struggle, and seem to grin, and then play dead. "Shsh," Andromeda kept telling him, but he went on whimpering and elbowing about until at last he was aloft. The air-travel appeared to soothe him. A mile from the village, on the brink of the enfolding hill, she plonked the basket down, lifted the hanky, and gave the little puppy a good talking-to, with much play of the raised forefinger, the stamped foot, the meaning frown. In fact the little puppy was so flummoxed and confused by this stage that he stared up at

Andromeda with candid incuriosity—and even yawned in her face. On they went, down into the ringed village. "Good day, good day," came the voices, and Andromeda sang songs at the top of her voice, lest the little puppy should unwarily choose to whinny or yelp. But the little puppy was very good and didn't make a sound. (To be quite honest, he was fast asleep.) When she reached the cabin Andromeda got up on tiptoe and peered in. Keithette was not about. Nor was Tom. So little Andromeda took the little puppy straight to her little room.

Now Andromeda had a lot of explaining to do (this had better be good!). And so, come to that, have we.

As things now stood, the village was the food of the dog —and the dog was, if not the worst of all possible dogs, then certainly the worst dog yet. The genetic policemen and bouncers that once kept species apart had loosened their hold on the living world. In less temperate zones than where lies our scene, there were creatures that limped and flapped in strange crevices between the old kingdoms, half fauna half flora, half insect half reptile, half bird half fish. Natural selection had given way to a kind of reverse discrimination —or tokenism. Any bloody fool of an amphibious parrot or disgraceful three-winged stoat had as much chance of survival, of success, as the slickest, the niftiest, the most singleminded dreck-eating ratlet or invincibly carapaced predator. Many human beings, too, were mildly dismayed to find themselves traveling backward down their evolutionary flarepaths—or, worse, sideways, into some uncharted humiliation of webs and pouches, of trotters and beaks. People, of whom there were few, tended to thin out near the deserts, of which there were plenty. In the deserts the lower forms flourished unchecked in their chaos: you could hardly turn your head without seeing some multipedic hyena or doubledecker superworm pulsing toward you over the mottled sands. The village lay to the north, not too far from the glasslands of ice. At these select latitudes, after its decades of inimical quiet, the planet earth was once again an hospitable, even a fashionable address. With so much food—with so much space and weather—nature had little selecting to do. Until the dog.

Perhaps the dog, then, was the Natural Selector. The dog was eight feet long and four feet high, very lumpily put together, the rolling, snapping head loosely joined to the top-heavy shoulders. In place of a tail he sported an extra limb, bare tibia, tendon and talon—quite useless, and far from decorative. His eyes were a scurvy yellow, his saliva a loud crimson, venomous and also acidic, capable of entirely dissolving human bones. The dog was the beneficiary of a new symbiotic arrangement whereby he healthily played host to several serious but by now ineffective diseases, his numerous parasites having (in this case) taken on rather more than they could handle. In times of yore the dog ate pretty well anything he could keep down, like a shark. These days, though, he was exclusively, even religiously homovorous. He looked bad on his diet. There never was a clearer demonstration of the fact that you shouldn't eat human beings. The dog's chief personal breakthrough was his coat, which was thick, patchy, fungoid and yet synthetic-looking, too shiny, like rayon or lurex. He was the first dog to earn a crust, to eke out a living in the northern lands. The village was his food. He seemed to need about one human being a week. He wasn't all that greedy, and human beings, he found, went a long way.

Nobody in the village had any idea what to do about the dog. Well, they had their shameful strategy; but it wasn't working. Idlers in a rejuvenated world, they had long lost the noble arts of survival and advantage, let alone fighting and killing. No one knew how to raise hell anymore. They milked the land of its rich life: indeed, some of the plants were as nutritious and sanguinary as meat itself; yes, many plants bled. They used few tools, and no weapons. Even fire they hoped soon to foreswear. This was the way the world was now.

For the next couple of days the little puppy was so very poorly that Andromeda was able to keep him bedded down in her clothes cupboard without much fear of detection. Sometimes, in a trance of foreboding, she found herself on the brink of resigning herself to the loss of her new friend. "Stay," she would whisper to him urgently. "Don't leave me. Stay, oh please *stay.*" At night Andromeda brought the little puppy a selection of juicy vegetables and encouraged him to eat. He seemed grateful for the sympathy, for the comfort, but turned away from the food, and sighed his long-suffering sigh. Then on the third day . . . Well, Andromeda was slowly eating breakfast with Keithette and Tom, her mother and "father." In the silence the sun played

subatomic ball with the moody motes of dust. Both Andromeda and Tom were eying Keithette a little warily. No
one had spoken with any freedom that morning, because
Keithette had yet to select and announce her mood-day.
There were seven to chose from (all different now, all sad
days, since the dog): Shunday, Moanday, Tearsday,
Woundsday, Thirstday, Fireday, Shatterday. . . . Tom
was crushing henna into a mortar bowl and saying, "I prefer
the single braid anyway."

"Why?" asked Keithette pitilessly. She was a rosy,
broad-faced woman, stocky and flat-chested (the standard
female form these days); but at such moments her mouth
looked as thin as a fissure in glass. "Why? Please tell me,
Tom."

Tom laid aside his pestle and made a two-handed gesture
of shaping. "Perhaps because it shows—it shows the essen-
tial oneness of your nature."

This was a bit much for Keithette. "*What* oneness?" she
said, and folded her arms tightly. "Go on. *What* oneness?"

And now Tom, too, was stumped. "I don't really know,"
he said. "But I'm sure that ribbon looks very nice with the
dress."

Keithette may have been about to soften. We shall never
know. At that moment, just as Andromeda watchfully
raised the wooden spoon to her lips—they heard a distinct
little bark from beyond the kitchen door. . . . The three
figures reared and stiffened. Time went on for a while with
nothing happening inside it, and the moment might well
have passed intact if there hadn't come a second yelp, more
emboldened and demanding than the first. Andromeda's

alarm was acute. She made to speak but was quickly checked by an unpierceable glare from her mother. Then came the third yelp.

"Shatterday," said Keithette.

But now she rose up, seeming to swell and take fire with the woman's need to confront the worst. Keithette strode to the passage door, Andromeda and Tom a couple of feet behind her. She turned, resolute and incensed, before she seized the handle. The door opened like a lid.

And what should they see but the little puppy, quite recovered, full of beans in fact, only briefly startled and now skipping and twisting, feinting this way and that, and wagging his tail with such violence that his entire rear end was just a furry little blur. Then he swooned onto his back with his cocked paws aloft. Andromeda burst out crying and pushed herself through to kneel at the little puppy's side.

"What's *that?*" said Keithette.

"Leave him alone," said Andromeda. "He's a little— 'puppy,'" she explained, with a new effort showing in her eyes. "A little *puppy.*"

Adorably the little puppy gazed upward.

"*My* little puppy," said Andromeda.

"Why do I put up with her?" Keithette began. "Answer me, Tom. Please answer me. Where did it come from? Right from the start she never gave me a moment's peace. Why can't she be like any other little girl? Why? Why? That's right. I'll pack you off to live with the children. Or the Queers! Where did you find it? Now you listen to me, Andromeda. *Andromeda,* indeed. Her own name's not good enough for her. She has to go and call herself Andromeda! What's it doing now? Well, I'll tell you one thing, young lady. It's not staying *here*."

It took many hours of supplication, many Blametakes and Faultfinds, and much work for Tom on the mat, over the tub, and in the sack, great play being made with the hot towels and cold compresses, the back scratchers and skin loofahs, not to mention all the hair stroking, neck nuzzling, and breast kissing—plus the tireless and tearful pleas of tiny Andromeda—but in the end Keithette was pretty well won over to the little puppy's presence, a presence that was understood to be temporary, contingent, multiprovisoed. Naturally, the ruling could be reversed at a single snap of Keithette's brawny red fingers. Ah, but what could you do when it came to a little puppy like this one, with his ridiculous frown and his beseeching eyes? All the little puppy had going for him, really, was his adorability. And he was adorable—yes he *was*. After the countless promises and penances, the clauses and covenants of the long afternoon, Keithette herself seemed quite exhausted by the fray.

"All right," she said. "It can live here for a while."

"*He*," said Andromeda.

"Where is it anyway?"

Where was the little puppy? Snuggling at Keithette's feet, of course, and blinking up at her gratefully. By nightfall the little puppy was ensconced on Keithette's lap. It was all Andromeda could do to prize him free for a cuddle. Tom looked on from his leisurebench with hard-won relief. He monitored Keithette for signs of sudden mood swing or

theme change. Everything seemed all right for now. But it
had been some Shatterday.


Oiled, groomed, distinctly plump, and impeccably toilet
trained, the little puppy was nowadays to be found, more
often than not, on his favorite perch: the window ledge in
Andromeda's little bedroom. Through the mists of the half
curtain, his tail wagging uncertainly, then quickening in
sudden bursts of recognition or general enthusiasm, the
little puppy watched the people come and go, for hours on
end. Because the people—the people were so beautiful! The
women striding about with their hands on their hips, occasionally pausing to talk and nod among themselves, arms
folded. The girls, regal and remote, with expensive self-
awareness in oval cheeks and artful hair. All colors and sizes
the people were. Yes, and the old, too, with their more
careful tread (easy does it), and the way light seemed to pour
from their human eyes. The little boys were stern and
watchful, shut-faced, on their guard. Why weren't they
playing? wondered the little puppy, in his way. Why
weren't they playing—bounding and tumbling like packs
of puppies?
    No one played except the little puppy. But the little
puppy played a lot. The jumping games, the rolling games,
the hiding games. He very nearly exasperated his young
mistress with these endless larks and sprees of his. One quiet
Shunday she found the little puppy frenziedly prying at a
round red bauble fixed (by Tom) to the foot of her bed.
Encouraged by his barking she managed to free the thing

from its clasp; she then rolled it into the little puppy's path. A ball, a red ball! The little puppy proceeded to chase it around the room. And he chased it around the room. And he chased it around the room again. Holding the ball in his jaws, he challenged Andromeda to shake it free and then throw it for him. Then he retrieved it and bounced around her until she threw it again. Really, the hysteria of the little puppy at such moments. Andromeda didn't understand. But the little puppy clearly needed his play, as badly as he needed his love and his food. Now, when she brought him his vegetables and fruit, the little puppy often thrust his whole head into the bowl.

Some passing people stared in once, and saw the little puppy on his perch. He yelped at them playfully, and tensed, hair-triggering himself for a romp. The people recoiled in hostile amazement. A small crowd gathered, and after a while, even though the little puppy had by now hidden himself under the bed, there came a stubborn thumping on the back door. This shuffling posse was confronted by Keithette—who settled their hash with a fearful blast. Andromeda was then called into the parlor to join Keithette and Tom in a three-hour discussion. The subject: Keithette's imagination. At this point, however, Andromeda resolved to act boldly.

With Tom's help and collusion, she fashioned a little collar for the little puppy—and a little leash. And out she walked into the village with him. Twisting and writhing and half-throttling himself at first, the little puppy soon fell into an obedient trot, only the head busy and indocile, bolting all shapes and colors as if the whole world might be food. It must be said that the experiment was not an obvious success. Many people jeered, or backed away, or burst into tears, and the little puppy himself gave a whine from some sluice in his sinuses, a whine of dismay at the unhappiness he somehow seemed to represent and personify. Andromeda walked on in full obstinacy and pride, the little puppy rather cowering now at her ankles. On their return—she could still hear the hecklers in her wake—Andromeda was greeted by Keithette who surprised everyone, including herself, by giving her daughter a smile of approval and by openly ruffling the shiny folds of the little puppy's neck. Andromeda adorned his collar with silver bells and took him out again the next day too. She had made up her mind. But the little puppy, it ought to be said, was a good deal daunted.

"I've got a name for you," Andromeda whispered in the dark. "Jackajack. Do you like it?" The little puppy was in bed with Andromeda. He liked it. He liked everything. "If you weren't an animal," she whispered, "I would call you John and you would be my boy." The little puppy gazed up at her, his eyes lit by an unbounded willingness.

Why do people love children? Why do children love babies? Why do we all love animals? What do animals love, that way? Everything, the whole world, more, even the stars up there—stars like the star called Andromeda, fixed in the scattered heavens, burning bright.


You couldn't really blame the villagers. They were all having a very bad time, and they weren't equipped for bad times. Whereas, in days gone by, the people would go about their tasks with tears of contentment in their eyes, now they wept the other tears. And where were they to turn? Down the soft decades they had lost the old get-up and go—the know-how, the make-do. Predation and all its paraphernalia had quite petered out of their gene cams and pulse codes. Given a generation or two, and given their new knack or curse of sudden *and* active adaptation, oh, I suppose they might have come up with something, in time. But there wasn't time.

They looked for authority, and what did they find? The natural leaders were, of course, the women with the loudest voices and the strongest personalities; and if you think Keithette is redoubtable enough, you should check out Clivonne—or Kevinia! At first they tried to hate the dog away. They sat around hating it and hating it, but still the dog lumbered in for his weekly debauch. They tried to cry the dog away, and that didn't work either. They tried ignoring it; but being ignored didn't make much odds to a dog like this dog. So there were more consultations. They didn't hold a meeting: it was simply a matter of a few dozen exhausted and terrified husbands—all the Toms and Tims and Tams—sprinting with messages from hut to hut. Incidentally, no one had ever decided any of this. It wasn't a reaction to the deep past. You see, there was no deep *memory*. This was just the way the world was now.

And so they asked death in through the back door, and let him feast on the malevolved, the beakmen and wingwomen, the furred or shelled or slippery beings with their expressions of stunned disgrace. It was subliminally decided

that everything was all their fault. Ah, the poor Queers.
. . . One Fireday, Andromeda took the little puppy that
could to the place where the malevolved often hung out; he
was tolerantly greeted, and even made much of by some old
hinny or heteroclite, who cosseted the puppy's coat with a
limp flippered hand. The little puppy took to the Queers,
as indeed he took to everyone. They were defeatist, lacka-
daisical, and inert: faulty survival machines, they knew they
weren't made to last. They knew they probably wouldn't be
selected, not in the end, not in that sense. And how few of
them there were now. Soon, thought Andromeda, the poor
Queers will be all used up. Then what? Only one outcome.
She considered ways of perhaps saving the little puppy, if it
came to that.

On the way home they were followed for a while by a
group of women who shrieked and chanted at the little
puppy, and made unpleasant faces, cowing him rather
badly. "Come on, Jackajack," said Andromeda loudly.
"Never mind them." So he jinked along beside her, glancing back uneasily over his dropped shoulders. But Andromeda did not glance back. She walked straight and true,
filling her given space. For Andromeda enjoyed an ambig-
uous prestige in the village; she certainly had rarity value.
It was partly to do with such things as her refusal to go and
live in the child pool, and the fact that she had changed her
own name. She had changed it from Briana—to Andromeda, if you please. But it was really all about beauty: beauty.
Nobody knew what people were supposed to look like anymore or could guess at the human forms they once had
graced. The women all rugged and ruddy and right; the

men all drab, effaced, annulled. And yet everyone has time for beauty, for art, for pattern and plan. We all come around to beauty in the end. As instinctively as the dog salivated with pleasure on encountering human remains in some patch of his own chaotic excretions (his heart soared like a hawk), so the people gazed at little Andromeda's round-eyed face, her dark clefts and latencies, and felt pride in the human molding.

"Look, Jackajack," she said. They had come to the edge of the crater, the core, the deep dish and its great query of fire. Now the flames ate the air, spitting and chewing and clearing their throats. No one fed the fire yet it burned anyway, with no fuel—but with fission, perhaps; perhaps fission's daughters lay trapped beneath the crust. Although the village was godless, the crater was agreed to be at least semisacred, and the people felt its codes, sensed its secrets with reluctant awe. Certainly no one went down there just for the hell of it. And now of course it served a different function. "Look, Jackajack," whispered Andromeda. Down in the contoured chasm, ringed by fire, some women were tethering an old Queer to the stake, ready for Shatterday. The little puppy barked. He didn't like fire. Nor did the dog. But the dog didn't mind fire *that* much. He could put up with it, if he had to.

Keithette sat heftily at the round table, micromonitored by Tom and Andromeda. Both had been present at the infor-mal, morning-long seminar that Keithette had convened. The subject: Keithette's sensibility. The really warm work of the afternoon, though, had fallen on Tom alone—a tight regime of scalp kneading, hair braiding, intertoe loofahing, and hourly sexual intercourse. It hadn't worked. Nothing worked now. Because tonight was a night of the dog. And now it seemed that every day was Shatterday.

True to Andromeda's prediction, the inevitable came to pass and soon the supply of Queers was pretty much exhausted. Actually they were picked off a lot quicker than anybody bargained for, because even the dog turned his nose up at some of them. He killed them all right, with one swipe of his bleeding claws, and gave the corpses a frightful worrying; but he wouldn't eat them. He just stood there, stupid and implacable, for hour after hour (he stayed upright at all times, even during his egregious naps), before tearing off the dead Queer's best limb and trudging away with it—to return the next night, and the next. Now he would peer down into the lit crater and see no offering for him there. Just the crackling fire, no louder or brighter than the fire of hunger in his heart.

"Here he comes," said Keithette.

Yes, here he comes. You could hear him liquidly snorting and yodeling as he loped toward them over the fields, nearer, ever nearer. The whole village listened—listened in darkness to a world of sound. His creaking gait, his grunts, his great gurglings at the prospect of messy satiation. Next, his long silence at the brink of the crater, his thwarted howl of disappointment, his final scream of ravenous rage. Then the sniffings and rootlings round the huts, the latherings and flappy droolings, the regular flinging of his bulk against any weakness, the splitting of wood, the human cries, the

heavy arhythmical bounding of the chase, the incensed rip-
pings and gulpings of the kill. . . . Once, as the dog was
fizzily consuming his prey, the little puppy (held fast on
Andromeda's lap) gave out a piercing yelp. Outside there
was sudden silence—followed, several minutes later, by a
growl of fabulous greed and hatred, inches from the front
door. But the dog's hunger had lost its rawness (and there'd
be another night), and all they heard then were the usual
sounds of grumbling haulage as the dog dragged the half-
eaten carcass out of the village and into the hills.

"He's going now," said Keithette. She closed her eyes
and wiggled a finger at Tom, who moved grimly toward
her. "When will the dog stop coming? When? When? Why
don't I know what to do? Why? Why? Tomorrow I'll speak
to Royene, and to Clivonne. I might even speak to Kevinia.
I don't know why, but I think I'll be the last to go. Not
there," she told Tom. "There. There."

When the danger of predation is great, communities of
whatever phylum tend to interknit more closely, and hier-
archical roles become sharper and more keenly contested.
Or at any rate that's the idea. This particular community,
for instance, had long lost all genetic heft. Probably their
best bet would have been to move out and go nomad for a
while. But site-tenacity was, alas, pretty well the only sta-
ble element in the local DNA transcription. How could you
run when, in your head, this was the only place?

With a square meal inside him, and a decent cadaver to
nibble and gnaw on, the dog would be gone for seven

nights. This seemed a clear gain, after the post-Queer chaos, and in fact everyone was secretly impressed by the dog's asceticism in restricting himself to one human per week. It would take him at least a couple of years to account for them all. That Shunday, however, brought unpleasant surprises.

On his last sortie the dog had forced his way into the spare-husband compound and selected his victim from the fifteen men who huddled there. In the skirmish three spare husbands had been wounded or nicked by the dog's teeth and claws. By Moanday afternoon they had swelled outlandishly in the belly and sprouted coarse hair on their backs and buttocks. All three died during the night, in speechless horror. On Woundsday it was reported that seven spare husbands who had merely come into contact with the dog's coat had developed cutaneous conditions of incredible virulence; they, too, passed away, in a frothing nightmare of serpigo and yaws. By Fireday the remaining four men— who had done no more than smell the dog's breath— checked out with toxic shock.

The women's thoughts naturally turned to the child pool, housed in a none too sturdy structure just behind the spare-husband compound. Well, I say "naturally," but it should be stressed that things had quieted down very noticeably on the bearing-and-caring circuit, the operative genes being, if not selfless, then fairly unambitious in tendency. So were they all meant to die, quickly, without a fight? Nothing wants to evolve but everyone wants to survive. We just don't want to go. Even when life is poor, and mostly fearful, and there are pressing reasons to quit—we don't want to. We don't want to go.

Again there was talk, and the sending of messages, and the distraught husbands making their rounds. At noon on Shatterday, as if by mass somnambulism, the entire village gathered in the crater by the swan-neck of fire. Yes, Andromeda was there with the little puppy, reflexively shielding him from the grimaces of the crowd. They all knew what was going to happen—knew it with exhausted shame, with a consciousness of falling far short of any human destiny. Royene and Clivonne presided over a stout barrel. The villagers then filed past, each of them dropping into the tub a personal possession—a scarf, a tool, a headband, an earring. There were no exceptions. Tom held the little puppy as Andromeda took her turn. At last Kevinia strode forward, looked around about her, and rolled up her sleeves, her hard face shining in the silent heat. It was at that moment that the little puppy barked—barked at Kevinia! He even started *growling*. Kevinia stared on, with scandalized disdain, as Andromeda fought to contain the little puppy, and with Tom's help eventually subdued her struggling, snapping charge. So it was with the extra radiance of flame-eyed rectitude that Kevinia reached into the barrel, held aloft and then, with a gesture of explanation, of disclosure, dropped to the ground the little red ball.


The sky said *war*. "War," declared the sky. Up above, the evening stars were sending light, the nuclear way, their fuel-counts stretched by vast equations, pulsar, quasar, giant, and dwarf—and Andromeda burning, too, in rich implosions, changing and charging through the electric firmament. Below, the clouds looked as hard and clearly etched as granite, the work of abrupt propulsions, strong interactions . . .

Now the little puppy lay in the arms of his mistress, for the last hours. His senses all had missions: to find a way through the veils of her grief and, perhaps, to help assuage it. His passionate vigilance also had an animal edge. You've seen those puppies at the playground or the seaside, tethered to a fence while the whole world romps and dances. This is the maximum puppy suffering; it stings far worse than hunger. But now the little puppy went through that pain to the other side, twisting and tugging within himself, just to hold the grief and make it lighter. "Thank you, Jackajack," Andromeda murmured, as she felt the hot squirmings—the unbounded willingness—of his love. Their little room held a blushful glow: early to bed in summer, curtailment, just exclusion. Andromeda had the pride to meet her fate, like a woman. But she didn't want to go. She thought of escape, of flight (no one would have stopped her), just herself and the little puppy. It was a big bare planet now, though, and very lonely. Great emptinesses pressed in on the human place. Andromeda had the pride. But she didn't want to go.

Soon they heard the apologetic whispers in the yard. Keithette sat at the round table, deep in her own drama. She would not, she would *never* say good-by. Tom looked up shyly (still tired and faint after four hours of unpunctuated cunnilingus). "I'm going now," said Andromeda, and she thought: What strange creatures we are— really. "I'm going now. Good-by, Jackajack," she said. "Stay. . . . Stay."

The dog was coming. Already you could sense his

maimed skirling as it poured forth, over the hills. Flanked by her two husbands, the burly Kevinia led Andromeda to the lip of the great concavity, down the widely looping path, down to where the fire was eating its meal of dusk. The ugly crucifix stood there waiting, like a Queer. Kevinia gave instructions. Number-one husband secured Andromeda's little hands, relying on number-two husband to bind her little feet. She looked from face to face, but nothing was said and they soon hurried away, back up the winding path. And so Andromeda stared at the fire, its sprites and genies and their pure pandemonium.

Unevenly the homovore sidled through the outskirts of the village, the heavy threads of saliva whirring—almost rattling—in savage nostalgia as he passed the site of some earlier kill or decisive mangling, the jaws slackly ajar and then cracking shut in a vestigial spasm, the nailed talons splitting and spoking on the bare earth. There he goes now, very horribly, the needled fur, the flapped and misshapen genitals, the fifth leg protruding from the rear like the aftermath of some deeply injudicious sexual exploit. The Natural Selector. Although resilient himself—he could pretty well boast pan-immunity—the dog was boiling and bursting with whole ecologies of trapped viruses, germs, and microbes: anthrax, foul brood, rinderpest, staggers, scours, glanders, hard pad, sheep rot, and mange. He shimmered like heat haze. The flowers were always dead where the dog had slept.

We all know the normal posture of the village when the dog was on its way. It played dead. In humiliated torpor it hid its human face. But on this night of sacrifice, of new nausea and defeat, the shouldered heads would not bow to receive their blows. Why? It was Andromeda, it was pride, it was beauty—was it also, perhaps, in some perverse way, the girl's championship of the little puppy? Now you could feel the low rumble of hot temper, of petulant mutiny. Among the clustered cabins, windows and even doors were thrown open, and husbands appeared, shouting and waving their arms, while the women, too, jeered and hated, trying and trying to hate the dog away.

Not that the dog seemed much abashed by this treatment. After a few stupid pauses and directionless snarls (the snarls like weary swearing), he moved on, toward the ring. Stupidly, he paused again, as some rogue cramp or seizure coursed through his system. In truth he looked far from well. His diet was surely getting to him. Yes, even the dog was capable of deteriorating on such a regime: these days he wasn't so friendly with his own emanations, and could deck himself with a single burp. . . . He came to the edge of the circle. With scarlet eyes he peered down through the distorted air—and saw a figure, ready at the stake. He grunted, and started down the track: this was good, this was more like it, this was the way things were supposed to be run. Halfway down he looked up and saw the emboldened villagers gathered at the crater's rim, all around him, full of noise and gesture. What's the big deal? the dog seemed to wonder, and turned, and stared down through the tips of the flames to inspect the sacrifice, confident that he would find the usual knucklewalker or nervously yawning throwback tethered to the post. When he saw the little brown limbs, writhing (as indeed everything was writhing down there), the dog's stomach thumped and rumbled, and a pint or two of smoking saliva slopped from his mouth. Slowly now, with anticipation, with due reverence, the dog moved down the curling track.

Andromeda watched him, through the fire. Why, the flames themselves seemed to want to consume the dog, reaching out for him with tongues and fingers—to consume, to transform, to chew him up and spit him out again, detoxified. One little flamelet couldn't resist, and leaned out to stoke the dog's fiery fur. The dog growled abstractedly as a stray patch of his coat briefly crackled like torched gorse. But he plodded on—he could take it—and at last nosed into the query of fire. When he saw Andromeda, when he smelled her, and sensed the quality of the provender staked out before him, his limbs galloped forward (the head and body lurching after them), before pulling to an untidy halt, twenty feet away. Now he paused again. The dog valued beauty, too, in his way. He was going to eat it very, very slowly.

Andromeda met his crimson eyes. Her personal bodyguards or body gods, her gods of swooning, wished to take her elsewhere and mother her into sleep. But with all the fever and magic down there in the ring—you couldn't block the hot oxygen, the performing blood. The fire hissed louder than the crowd, here in the burning pan. She saw the dog's jaw drop open: the carcinogenic teeth, the tumor of the tongue, the flamelets of sizzling drool. Then, as abruptly as an uppercut, the dog's mouth chopped shut, his head dipped, and he lumbered carefully toward her.

Who sensed it first, Andromeda or the dog? In retreating

waves the ringed crowd fell slowly silent, spherical music falling through the frequencies and dying on its band. The dog himself seemed struck by the orderly swooning hush. What was that they heard in the flame-flecked quiet? Was it the jink of tiny bells? With a painful twist of the neck the dog looked up at the crater's rim. On the brink of the curling path, the bright red ball in his mouth, stood the little puppy Jackajack.

He too had come to meet his destiny; and down he started, the little puppy, at a prancing trot, the front paws evenly outthrust, the head held pompously erect. The dog watched him with a loathing that bordered on fear. Yes, fear. Of course the dog was as brave as a lion, and a lot stupider; but everything fears its own reverse image, its antimatter or Antichrist. Everything fears itself. Salivating anew, and dully grunting, the dog watched as the little puppy (staring straight ahead) swanked his way down the wide spiral, disappeared behind the veils of flame, and strutted out into the ring. He marched straight up to the dog, right into his ambient miasma, dropped the red ball, skipped backward to crouch with his nose on his paws— and barked.

The dog hesitated, his eyes lit by a weak leer. This shrimp, this morsel, this starter: what was its game? The little puppy yelped again, jumping forward to straddle the ball, then sprang back to his posture of cocked entreaty. For several seconds the dog stared on in leaden surprise, his inner templates shuffling and dealing, looking for stalled memories, messages, codes. The crowd, too, mumbled in confusion, until someone started yelling, hooting—goading, goading the dog on. Now the little puppy dribbled the red ball into the dog's path and repeated his bouncing dance, with many a coquettish swivel and feint. Gruffly the dog pitched forward. But in a trice the little puppy swooped down on the ball and ran two sharp circles—then flopped to the ground with his back to the dog, kissing and nuzzling his incomparable prize. With his flooded mouth gaping the dog watched the puppy's tail sweep unconcernedly back and forth, saw the plump little buttocks tensed and tuned. Suddenly he pitched forward again—and the puppy was up and away, the ball held high as he sauntered out of range. Ooh, that little *puppy*—good enough to *eat*.

As the game continued, watched by the crowd and the excited fire (each with its own catcalls and applause), the dog seemed to be getting other ideas about the puppy, judging by the great palatinate extension craning from his warped nethers, his malarial eyes, and tempestuous breath. Now the little puppy had trotted some yards off and languished on his back with his paws upraised, the red ball apparently unregarded at his side. Stupidly, the dog sensed his moment. He came forward, hurdling into his run, picking up speed until, sure of triumph (though the face showed some alarm at his own ballistic daring), he launched himself heavily through the air. Of course the ball and the puppy had both disappeared—and the dog landed with such crunchy chaos on the smelted rock that the crowd momentarily winced into silence, wondering if the dog was dead or damaged, wondering to what fury he would now aspire when he awoke. . . . Seconds passed and the body never stirred. With a quick pining glance at Andromeda the little puppy approached the venomous heap, the steaming wreckage of the dog. No one breathed as the puppy sniffed and barked, and reached out a paw toward the dog's open mouth. He nosed about among growing murmurs of hope. Now the little puppy even raised a back leg and seemed about to . . . but it was Andromeda's cry that forewarned him. Although he jumped back with a squeal, the dog's claws had done their work, swiping a flash of blood onto the puppy's pink belly.

The dog was playing too: playing dead. But he wasn't playing anymore. Hugely he reared up on four legs, on two legs, and hugely he shook the bloody rags of his rage. Now the chase began, in earnest, the great dog bounding after the little puppy, in tightening circles, skidding and twisting, turned this way, that way, this, that. For a time the puppy seemed freer than air, whimsically lithe, subatomic, superluminary, all spin and charm, while the dog moved on rails like a bull, pure momentum and mass, and forever subject to their laws. It couldn't last. The puppy was always tumbling, as puppies will, and leaving blood on the earth, and looking weaker and smaller each time he mustered himself for the turn, with the dog seeming to fill all space, seeming to fill all hell and more. . . . At last the puppy led the dog into a wide arc at the end of the scythe of fire. Out they came, the large animal following the small, and gaining, gaining. "Turn," said the crowd. "Turn," said Andromeda, as they flashed past. The puppy could now feel the dog's hot breath on his rump, the bunsen of inflamed saliva and gums, and yet he tumbled and bounded on, seemingly propelled only by the desperate rhythm of his stride. Together they fast approached the great join of fire, almost one animal now, the puppy's tail tickling the frothing nose of the dog, whose jaws opened ready for the first seizing snap. Turn, turn—

"Turn," said Andromeda.

But the little puppy did not turn. With a howl of terror and triumph he hurled himself high into the flames—and the dog, like a blind missile, heat-seeking, like a weapon of spittle and blood, could only follow.

And so at last the flames settled down to eat. And what a meal they made of the dog. What coughing and gagging, what outrageous retching and hawking, what bursts and punctures of steam and gas, what eructations, what dis-gorgements—and the leaping plumes and flashes and puls-ing brain-scans the flames made, until they relaxed and quieted, and began to breathe again.

When Tom untethered her, Andromeda pushed past him and walked the length of the scythe of fire. She found the still-smoking body of the little puppy, belly-upward, just beyond the join of fire, and she knelt to cradle him in her arms. The flames hadn't wanted to eat him; they had wanted to bear him through and deliver him safely to the other side. Now the little puppy coughed, and flinched, and blinked up at her for the last time. Yes, the puppy music was fading. The little puppy could not persist, not in that little-puppy form—the singed tail, the blood on the delicate tummy, the poor paws limp now, holding no life. Andromeda looked up. The villagers had lined the curling path, silently. But as her grief began they too began to weep, to make moan, until the sounds, borne heavenward by the fire, drifted up into the fleeces of the sky.

Late that night Andromeda lay awake, her hot face pressed against the soaked pillow. Her thoughts, naturally, were with the little puppy Jackajack. She had carried his little body to the stake, and placed it there on a scarf of white. The villagers had all knelt in homage, and cursed themselves for shame that they had ever scorned or doubted the little puppy, the little puppy that could. There was grief and there was joy. And there was shame. Tomorrow the little puppy would lie in state, for the propitiations of the villagers. Then she would bury him outside the village, over the hills—by the nervous creek. But the scythe would be a sacred place, and everyone who passed there would always think of the little puppy. Now he is gone from life, she said to herself. And what does life look like without him? If he could drink all my tears, she murmured; if he could just lap them up. She thought of his face as he smiled at her for the last time—so gentle, full of such intimate forgiveness. Infinitely intimate, and lit by secrets, too.

Then she heard a soft tapping on her window, patient and remote. She climbed from the bed and looked out. All was dark and grieving. Andromeda wrapped herself in a shawl and went quickly to the passage. She opened the door and said,

"Jackajack?"

The boy stood there, against a swirl of stars, his body still marked by the claws and the flames. She reached up to touch the tears in his human eyes.

"John," she said.

His arms were strong and warlike as he turned and led her into the cool night. They stood together on the hilltop and gazed down at their new world.

# THE

---

# IMMORTALS

---

It's quite a prospect. Soon the people will all be gone and I will be alone forever. The human beings around here are in very bad shape, what with the solar radiation, the immunity problem, the rat-and-roach diet, and so on. They are the last; but they can't last (though try telling *them* that). Here they come again, staggering out to watch the hell of sunset. They all suffer from diseases and delusions. They all believe that they are . . . But let the poor bastards be. Now I feel free to bare my secret.

I am the Immortal.

Already I have been around for an incredibly long time. If time is money, then I am the last of the big spenders. And

you know, when you've been around for as long as I have,
the diurnal scale, this twenty-four-hour number, can really
start to get you down. I tried for a grander scheme of things.
And I had my successes. I once stayed awake for seven years
on end. Not even a nap. Boy, was I bushed. On the other
hand, when I was ill in Mongolia that time, I sacked out for
a whole decade. At a loose end, cooling my heels in a Saharan
oasis, for eighteen months I picked my nose. On one occasion—when there was nobody around—I teased out a lone
handjob for an entire summer. Even the unchanging croco-
diles envied my baths in the timeless, in the time-mottled
rivers. Frankly, there wasn't much else to do. But in the
end I ceased these experiments and tamely joined the night-
day shuttle. I seemed to need my sleep. I seemed to need to
do the things that people seemed to need to do. Clip my
nails. Report to the can and the shaving basin. Get a hair-
cut. All these *distractions*. No wonder I never got anything
done.

   I was born, or I appeared or materialized or beamed
down, near the city of Kampala, Uganda, in Africa. Of
course, Kampala wasn't there yet, and neither was Uganda.
Neither was Africa, come to think of it, because in those
days the land masses were all conjoined. (I had to wait until
the twentieth century to check a lot of this stuff out.) I
think I must have been a dud god or something; conceivably
I came from another planet which ticked to a different clock.
Anyway I never amounted to much. My life, though long,
has been largely feckless. I had to hold my horses for quite
a while before there were any human beings to hang out
with. The world was still cooling. I sat through geology,

waiting for biology. I used to croon over those little warm ponds where space-seeded life began. Yes, I was there, cheering you on from the touchline. For my instincts were gregarious, and I felt terribly lonely. And hungry.

Then plants showed up, which made a nice change, and certain crude lines of animal. After a while I twigged and went carnivorous. Partly out of self-defense I became a prodigious hunter. (It was hardly a matter of survival, but nobody likes being sniffed and clawed and chomped at the whole time.) There wasn't an animal they could dream up that I couldn't kill. I kept pets, too. It was a healthy kind of outdoors life, I suppose, but not very stimulating. I yearned for . . . for reciprocation. If I thought the Permian age was the pits it was only because I hadn't yet lived through the Triassic. I can't tell you how dull it all was. And then, before I knew it—this would have been about 6,000,000 B.C.—the first (unofficial) Ice Age, and we all had to start again, more or less from scratch. The Ice Ages, I admit, were considerable blows to my morale. You could tell when one was coming: there'd be some kind of cosmic lightshow, then, more often than not, a shitstorm of moronic impacts; then dust, and pretty sunsets; then darkness. They happened regularly, every seventy thousand years, on the dot. You could set your watch by them. The first Ice Age took out the dinosaurs, or so the theory goes. I know different. They could have made it, if they'd tightened their belts and behaved sensibly. The tropics were a little stifling and gloomy, true, but perfectly habitable. No, the dinosaurs had it coming: a very bad crowd. Those lost-world adventure movies got the dinosaurs dead right. Incredibly stupid, incredibly touchy—and incredibly *big*. And always brawling. The place was like a whaling yard. I was onto fire by then, of course, and so I ate well. It was burgers every night.

The first batch of ape-people were just a big drag as far as I was concerned. I was pleased to see them, in a way, but mostly they were just a hassle. All that evolution—and for this? It was a coon's age before they ever amounted to anything, and even then they were still shockingly grasping and paranoid. With my little house, my fur suits, my clean-shaven look, and my barbecues, I stood out. Occasionally I became the object of hatred, or worship. But even the friendly ones were no use to me. *Ugh. Ich. Akk.* What kind of conversation do you call that? And when at last they improved, and I made a few pals and started having relationships with the women, along came a horrible discovery. I thought they would be different, but they weren't. They all got old and died, like my pets.

As they are dying now. They are dying all about me.

At first, around here, we were pleased when the world started getting warmer. We were pleased when things started brightening up again. Winter is always depressing —but nuclear winter is somehow especially grim. Even I had wearied of a night that lasted thirteen years (and New Zealand, I find, is pretty dead at the best of times). For a while, sunbathing was all the rage. But then it went too far in the other direction. It just kept on getting hotter—or rather there was a change in the nature of the heat. It didn't feel like sunlight. It felt more like gas or liquid: it felt like rain, very thin, very hot. And buildings don't seem to hold it off properly, even buildings with roofs. People stopped being sun-worshipers and started being moon-worshipers. Life became nightlife. They're fairly cheerful, considering —sorrier for others than they are for themselves. I suppose it's lucky they can't tell what's really coming down.

The poor mortals, I grieve for them. There's just nothing they can do about that molten fiend up there in the middle of the sky. They faced the anger, then they faced the cold; and now they're being nuked all over again. Now they're being renuked, doublenuked—by the slow reactor of the sun.

Apocalypse happened in the year A.D. 2045. When I was sure it was coming I headed straight for the action: Tokyo. I'll come right out and say that I was pretty much ready to quit. Not that I was particularly depressed or anything. I certainly wasn't as depressed as I am now. In fact I had recently emerged from a five-year hangover and, for me, the future looked bright. But the planet was in desperate shape by then and I wanted no part of it anymore. I wanted out. Nothing else had ever managed to kill me, and I reckoned that a direct hit from a nuke was my only chance. I'm cosmic —in time—but so are nukes: in power. If a nuke hasn't the heft to blow me away (I said to myself), well, nothing else will. I had one serious misgiving. The deployment fashion at that time was for carpet detonations in the hundred-kiloton range. Personally I would have liked something a

little bigger, say a megaton at least. I missed the boat. I
should have grabbed my chance in the days of atmospheric
tests. I always used to kick myself about that sixty-meg
sonofabitch the Soviets tried out in Siberia. Sixty million
tons of TNT: surely not even I would have walked away
from that. . . .

I leased a top-floor room at the Century Inn near Tokyo
Tower, bang in the middle of town. I wanted to take this
one right on the nose. At the hotel they seemed to be glad
of my custom. Business was far from brisk. Everybody knew
it would start ending here: it started ending here a century
ago. And by this time cities everywhere were all dying
anyway. . . . I had my money on an airburst, at night. I
bribed the floor guard and he gave me access to the roof: the
final sleepout. The city writhed in mortal fear. Me, I
writhed in mortal hope. If that sounds selfish, well, then I
apologize. But who to? When I heard the sirens and the air-
whine I sprang to my feet and stood there, nude, on tiptoe,
with my arms outstretched. And then it came, like the
universe being unzipped.

First off, I must have taken a lot of prompt radiation,
which caused major headaches later on. At the time I
thought I was being tickled to death by Dionysus. Simul-
taneously also I was zapped by the electromagnetic pulse
and the thermal rush. The EMP you don't have to worry
about. Take it from me, it's the least of your difficulties.
But the heat is something else. These are the kind of temperatures that turn a human being into a wall-shadow. Even
I took a bit of a shriveling. Although I can joke about it
now (it ain't half hot, Mum; phew, what a scorcher!), it

really was rather alarming at the time. I couldn't breathe and I blacked out—another first: I didn't die but at least I fainted. For quite a while, too, because when I woke up everything had gone. I'd slept right through the blast, the conflagration, the whole death typhoon. Physically I felt fine. Physically I was, as they say, in great shape. I was entirely purged of that hangover. But in every other sense I felt unusually low. Yes, I was definitely depressed. I still am. Oh, I act cheerful, I put on a brave face; but often I think that this depression will never end—will see me through until the end of time. I can't think of anything that's really very likely to cheer me up. Soon the people will all be gone and I will be alone forever.

They are sand people, dust people, people of dust. I'm fond of them, of course, but they're not much company. They are deeply sick and deeply crazy. As they diminish, as they ebb and fade, they seem to get big ideas about themselves. Between you and me, I don't feel too hot either. I look good, I look like my old self; but I've definitely felt better. My deal with diseases, incidentally, is as follows: I get them, and they hurt and everything, yet they never prove fatal. They move on, or I adapt. To give you a comparatively recent example, I've had AIDS for seventy-three years. Just can't seem to shake it.

An hour before dawn and the stars still shine with their new, their pointed brightness. Now the human beings are all going inside. Some will fall into a trembling sleep. Others will gather by the polluted well and talk their bullshit all day long. I will remain outside for a little while, alone, under the immortal calendar of the sky.


Classical antiquity was interesting (I suppose I'm jumping on ahead here, but you're not missing much). It was in Caligulan Rome that I realized I had a drink problem. I began spending more and more of my time in the Middle East, where there was always something happening. I got the hang of the economic masterforces and flourished as a Mediterranean trader. For me, the long hauls out to the Indies and back were no big deal. I did good but not great, and by the eleventh century I'd popped up again in Central Europe. In retrospect that now looks like a mistake. Know what my favorite period was? Yes: the Renaissance. You really came good. To tell you the truth, you astonished me. I'd just yawned my way through five hundred years of disease, religion, and zero talent. The food was terrible. Nobody looked good. The arts and crafts stank. Then—pow! And all at once like that, too. I was in Oslo when I heard what was happening. I dropped everything and was on the next boat to Italy, terrified I'd miss it. Oh, it was heaven. Those guys, when they painted a wall or a ceiling or whatever—it stayed painted. We were *living* in a masterpiece over there. At the same time, there was something ominous about it, from my point of view. I could see that, in every sense, you were capable of anything. . . . And after the Renaissance what do I get? Rationalism and the industrial revolution. Growth, progress, the whole petrochemical stampede. Just as I was thinking that no century could possibly be dumber than the nineteenth, along comes the twentieth. I swear, the entire planet seemed to be staging some kind of stupidity contest. I could tell then how the human story would end. Anybody could. Just the one outcome.

My suicide bids date back to the Middle Ages. I was forever throwing myself off mountains and stuff. Boulder overcoats and so on. They never worked. Christ, I've been hit by lightning more times than I care to remember, and lived to tell the tale. (I once copped a meteorite full in the face; I had quite a job crawling out from under it, and felt off-color all afternoon.) And this was on top of fighting in innumerable wars. Soldiering was my passion for millennia —you saw the world—but I started to go off it at the beginning of the fifteenth century. I who had fought with Alexander, with the great Khans, suddenly found myself in a little huddle of retching tramps; across the way was another little huddle of retching tramps. That was Agincourt. By Passchendaele war and I were through. All the improvisation—all the know-how and make-do—seemed to have gone out of it. It was just death, pure and simple. And my experiences in the nuclear theater have done nothing to restore the lost romance. . . . Mind you, I was slowly losing interest in everything. Generally I was becoming more reclusive and neurotic. And of course there was the booze. In fact, halfway through the twentieth century my drink problem got right out of hand. I went on a bender that lasted for ninety-five years. From 1945 to 2039—I was smashed. A metropolitan nomad, I lived by selling off my past, by selling off history: Phoenician knickknacks, He-

brew scrolls, campaign loot—some of it was worth a bomb.
I fell apart. I completely lost my self-respect. I was like the
passenger on the crippled airplane, with the duty-free upended over my mouth, trying to find the state where nothing matters. This was how the whole world seemed to be
behaving. And you cannot find this state. Because it doesn't
exist. Because things do matter. Even here.

Tokyo after the nuclear attack was not a pretty sight. An
oily black cake with little brocades of fire. My life has been
crammed with death—death is my life—but this was a new
wrinkle. Everything had gone. Nothing was happening.
The only light and activity came from the plasma-beams
and nukelets that were still being fired off by some splutter-
ing satellite or rogue submarine. What are they *doing*, I
asked myself, shooting up the graveyard like this? Don't
ask me how I made it all the way down here to New Zealand.
It is a long story. It was a long journey. In the old days, of
course, I could have walked it. I had no plans. Really I just
followed the trail of life.

I rafted my way to the mainland and there was nothing
there either. Everything was dead. (To be fair, a lot of it had
been dead already.) Occasionally, as I groped my way south,
I'd see a patch of lichen or a warped mushroom, and later a
one-legged cockroach or an eyeless rat or something, and
that lifted my spirits for a while. It was a good eighteen
months before I came across any human beings worth the
name—down in Thailand. A small fishing community
sheltered by a cusp in the coastal mountains and by freak

wind conditions (freak wind conditions being the only kind of wind conditions there were at that time). The people were in a bad way, naturally, but still hauling odds and ends out of the sea—you wouldn't call them fish exactly. I begged for a boat and they wouldn't give me one, which was understandable. I didn't want to argue about it, so I just hung around until they all died. That didn't take too long. I had about a four-year wait, if I remember correctly. Then I loaded up and pushed off and didn't care where the hell the winds took me. I just pushed off into the dying sea, hoping for life.

And I found it, too, after a fashion, down here among the dust people. The last. I'd better make the most of these human beings, because they're the only human beings I've got left. I mourn their passing. What is it to want others, to want others to be?

Once, finding myself in ancient China with plenty of cash and a century to kill, I bought a baby elephant and raised her from infant to invalid. I called her Babalaya. She lived for a hundred and thirteen years and we had time to get to know each other quite well. The larky way she tossed her head about. Her funny figure: all that bulk, and no ass (from the rear she looked like a navvy, slumped over the bar in a Dublin pub). Babalaya—only woman I ever cared a damn about. . . . No, that's not true. I don't know why I say that. But long-term relationships have always been difficult for me and I've tended to steer clear of them. I've only been married three or four thousand times—I'm not the kind to keep lists—and I shouldn't think my kids are even up there in the five figures. I had gay periods, too. I'm sure, though, that you can see the problem. I am used to watching mountains strain into the sky, or deltas forming. When they say that the Atlantic or whatever is sinking by half an inch a century, I *notice* these things. There I am, shacked up with some little honey. I blink—and she's a boiler. While I remained stranded in my faultless noon, time seemed to be scribbling all over everybody right in front of my eyes: they would shrink, broaden, unravel. I didn't mind that much, but the women couldn't handle it at all. I drove those broads crazy. "We've been together for twenty years," they'd say: "How come I look like shit and you don't?" Besides, it wasn't smart to hang around too long in any one place. Twenty years was pushing it. And I did push it, many, many times, on account of the kids. Apart from that I just had flings. You think one-night stands are pretty unsatisfactory? Imagine what I think of them. For me, twenty years is a one-night stand. No, not even. For me, twenty years is a knee-trembler. . . . And there were unpleasant complications. For instance, I once saw a granddaughter of mine coughing and limping her way through the Jerusalem *soukh*. I recognized her because she recognized me; she let out a harsh yell, pointing a finger which itself bore a ring I'd given her when she was little. And now she was little all over again. I'm sorry to say that I committed incest pretty regularly in the very early days. There was no way around incest, back then. It wasn't just me: everyone was into it. A million times I have been bereaved, and then another million. What pain I have known, what megatons of pain. I miss them all—how I miss them. I miss my Babalaya. But you'll understand that relationships of every kind are bound to be fairly strained (there will be tensions) when one party is mortal and the other is not.

The only celebrity I ever knew at all well was Ben Jonson, in London at that time, after my return from Italy. Ben and I were drinking buddies. He was boisterous in his cups, and soppy too, sometimes; and of course he was very blue about the whole Shakespeare thing. Ben used to sit through that guy's stuff in tears. I saw Shakespeare once or twice, in the street. We never met, but our eyes did. I always had the feeling that he and I might have hit it off. I thought the world of Shakespeare. And I bet I could have given him some good material.

Soon the people will all be gone and I will be alone forever. Even Shakespeare will be gone—or not quite, because his lines will live in this old head of mine. I will have the companionship of memory. I will have the companionship of dreams. I just won't have any people. It's true that I had those empty years before the human beings arrived, so I'm used to solitude. But this will be different, with nobody to look forward to at the end of it.

There is no weather now. Days are just a mask of fire— and the night sky I've always found a little samey. Before, in the early emptiness, there were pets, there were plants, there were nature rambles. Well, there's nothing much to ramble in now. I *saw* what you were doing to the place. What was the matter? Was it too *nice* for you or something?

Jesus Christ, you were only here for about ten minutes. And look what you did.

Grouped around the poisoned well, the people yawn and mumble. They are the last. They have tried having kids— I have tried having kids—but it doesn't work out. The babies that make it to term don't look at all good, and they can't seem to work up any immunity. There's not much immunity around as it is. Everybody's low.

They are the last and they are insane. They suffer from a mass delusion. Really, it's the craziest thing. They all believe that they are—that they are eternal, that they are immortal. And they didn't get the idea from me. I've kept my mouth shut, as always, out of settled habit. I've been discreet. I'm not one of those wellside bores who babble on about how they knew Tutankhamen and scored with the Queen of Sheba or Marie Antoinette. They think that they will live forever. The poor bastards, if they only knew.

I have a delusion also, sometimes. Sometimes I have this weird idea that I am just a second-rate New Zealand schoolmaster who never did anything or went anywhere and is now painfully and noisily dying of solar radiation along with everybody else. It's strange how palpable it is, this fake past, and how human: I feel I can almost reach out and touch it. There was a woman, and a child. One woman. One child. . . . But I soon snap out of it. I soon pull myself together. I soon face up to the tragic fact that there will be no ending for me, even after the sun dies (which should at least be quite spectacular). I am the Immortal.

Recently I have started staying out in the daylight. Ah, what the hell. And so, I notice, have the human beings.

We wail and dance and shake our heads. We crackle with cancers, we fizz with synergisms, under the furious and birdless sky. Shyly we peer at the heaven-filling target of the sun. Of course, I can take it, but this is suicide for the human beings. Wait, I want to say. Not yet. Be careful— you'll hurt yourselves. Please. Please try and stay a little longer.

Soon you will all be gone and I will be alone forever.

I . . . I am the Immortal.